CROWN OF STARS AND FATE

BLOOD AND SALT BOOK THREE

ALEXIS CALDER

CW01497592

ILLARIA PUBLISHING

Cover Art by Fay Lane

Editing by Court of Spice

Editing by Fae Writer

Proofreading by BAH

 Created with Vellum

For everyone who had to make friends with their demons.

KINGDOM OF
BLOOD AND SALT

1

ARA

MY VISION FADED in and out, the blur of sleep taking longer than usual to dissipate so I could focus. Flickering lights sparkled all around me and I held my breath while I scanned my environment. The single window to my left only showed a dark, unfamiliar landscape. I could make out the silhouettes of trees and see the stars dusting the night sky, but nothing beyond. I had no idea where I was. And I had no idea how I'd gotten here.

"Ara?" Ryvin's voice was more tentative than I'd ever heard it; my name was spoken like a prayer.

My heart leaped at the sound, my body reacting to his presence with eager anticipation before it was suddenly squashed by an invisible wall. I tensed, retreating from him. Confused, I struggled to come to terms with the war within my own body.

"Where am I?" Why was I reacting this way?

He hesitated in the doorway. "Do you remember what happened?"

I shook my head.

"Oh, good, she's awake," Laera said, joining her brother in the doorway. "Now I don't have to listen to you blaming me for her death for the rest of our lives."

The princess pushed her way past her brother and crossed the room before sitting down on the bed next to me. "What's wrong with you? You look like you saw a ghost."

"She doesn't remember," Ryvin supplied.

"I see." Laera studied me, then turned to her brother. "At least that explains why she hasn't ripped you to shreds. Not that she could anymore without her magic."

Her words slammed into me like a wave crashing to shore and my eyes widened, taking in the man I thought I'd fallen in love with.

I remembered. The minotaur, the destruction, the loss... Balen was gone. All the tributes were gone. We'd released a goddess set on revenge and then Ryvin took everything from me.

"I'm sorry," he said.

"You betrayed me." My chest felt like it might cave in. If he'd asked, if only he'd asked, I'd have given him everything. Anything. Instead, he took. He stole. Had anything he said been real? "You used me."

Laera smoothed my hair and made a clicking sound that was probably supposed to be soothing. Without taking her gaze from me, she addressed her brother. "You need to leave."

I glared at him as shadows swirled around him, masking him from view. I didn't take my eyes off the darkness filling the hall until the door closed, leaving me alone with the princess of Konos.

"He fucked up," Laera said after a long pause. "But that doesn't mean we can't finish what we started. It'll be easier with his help, but if you want me to send him after his mother while us girls take on my father, I will kick his ass off Naxos so fast his head spins."

I looked at her, taking in the serious expression on her face. Somehow, in our few days of training together, it seemed we'd become friends. "You didn't know he was going to take my magic?"

She shook her head. "I never thought he'd do such a thing. I suspected he was your mate, but after what happened to his mother..." she sighed. "I guess it goes to show you can't trust anyone. Not even your mate."

"We're on Naxos?" I couldn't think about Ryvin right now. Or my stolen magic. Not yet.

"And the sooner we get away, the better in my opinion. Those Maenads freak me the fuck out." She shuddered. "And Dion is always trying to get me in his bed."

"I am not marrying him." I stood, my head spinning so much I had to sit back down.

"Don't worry, he's not stupid enough to cross Ryvin. I suppose that's the perk of what he did. Nobody is going to risk challenging someone with his shadows and your magic."

"Even you?" I asked.

She pressed her lips together. "We'll figure that out as we go. For now, just know that in this situation, I chose your side and I'm loyal until you cross me."

"I don't plan on crossing you. I don't even know what's

going on." I stood again, moving more slowly this time. It felt good to move my body.

"I thought the gods were going to take you down right there." She shook her head. "I can't believe Nyx didn't defend you after you helped her. But that's the gods for you. A bunch of selfish bastards."

My brow furrowed as I replayed the events in the labyrinth, and I looked down at my arms expecting to see the blood I'd spilled. It was gone. Someone had cleaned me up, brought me to Naxos. How long was I here? What kind of destruction happened while I was tucked safely away?

"The king is still alive, and Nyx won't help us. Am I remembering that correctly?" I swallowed over the lump in my throat. "It was all for nothing. We killed the monster, and we freed Nyx, but all the tributes are dead." *And I should be dead.* A hollow, empty ache expanded within me.

"In theory, we weakened my father, so there's a better chance of taking him down. But since Nyx couldn't do it, we're going to have to come up with a new plan. He's still going to be difficult to kill," Laera said.

"And Nyx?" I asked, almost afraid to know the answer.

"No idea, but we haven't seen the sun return yet."

"We have to get to Athos," I blurted. "She said she was going to take revenge on the humans. We have to warn my family. Make sure they're prepared."

"If she's on her way there, there's not much we can do," Laera said with a shrug.

"No, that's not an option. There has to be something," I replied. "I need to see Ryvin."

"You sure?" Laera asked.

I nodded. A gnawing sense of anger and righteousness

was slowly seeping into the void where my magic had been. "Alone."

"While I certainly approve of that look in your eyes, I want to remind you that you're essentially human now. I don't know what kind of impact taking your magic had on him. I don't know if my father's lack of concern for others was a result of his actions or if he was always like that. But I know there are rules and reasons why we can't siphon the magic from others unless it's our mate. It's not meant to be done."

"I'm not afraid of Ryvin," I said.

"I think that's part of the problem. You both should have been afraid of each other and instead, you decided to fall for each other." She shook her head. "This is the mess that happens when emotions get the better of you."

A gentle knock sounded on the door and we both whipped our heads toward it just as it opened.

Ryvin looked in, his expression pleading. "I'll leave if you tell me to. I'll leave the island if you want. But please, give me five minutes first."

"You don't have to talk to him, Ara," Laera said.

"It's alright," I told her.

Laera nodded, then walked silently toward the door, and after shooting a glare at her brother, she slipped out, leaving me alone with my mate.

He was pale, with purple circles under his eyes. Hair mussed; clothes wrinkled. I'd never seen him in such a state. Not that it mattered. It seemed to make him more attractive. I hated that there was a part of me that wanted to tug that tunic right over his head and throw him onto the bed.

I moved toward the wall, away from the bed, to reduce the temptation. "You had no right to do what you did."

"It was the only way to save you. I hate myself for it and I know that you hate me, but I will spend the rest of my life making it up to you," he said.

"You could have asked me. You could have included me in your plans. Instead, you stole it from me. You never gave me a choice or an option. How could you do that to me? After everything. How could you?"

"Because you would have said no."

"You don't know that. You didn't even give me a chance," I countered.

"It's not natural to share our magic. If you knew it was coming, the magic would have created a shield to keep it within you once I took a little bit of it. I wouldn't have been able to take it.

"I've spent years researching this, trying to figure out what went on between my mother and father, trying to help her, and trying to understand how she couldn't have seen it coming. Trust me, if I asked, your magic would have guarded itself and you would be dead."

"That was my choice to make." I glared at him. "You don't know how I'd have reacted. You should have included me."

"You can hate me all you want, but I was not about to let you die. I swore to you that I would always protect you, and that is what I did. You get to go back to your kingdom, to your sisters, to your life. And if you hate me until the day you die, I hope it's a good long hate."

I took a step toward him, anger surging through my veins, my pulse pounding in my ears. "Fuck you. You took away my choice, but you did it after you made me trust you. After you made me fall for you. I loved you."

Ryvin sucked in a breath and all the color drained from his face. "You loved me?"

"I thought I did. But how could I love someone who lied to me?" My eyes burned from holding back tears. "I should have believed you when you told me you weren't good for me."

His jaw tensed and his gaze hardened. "I never lied to you. Everything I told you was the truth."

"No, I suppose you just hid things from me instead. Made me feel like I couldn't live without you. I fell in love with the man who killed my father, Ryvin. What kind of monster am I?" Tears streamed down my face.

"I swear to you, I only did what I thought I had to do to keep you alive. It's always been about keeping you safe," he said.

I could barely hear a word he was saying. My mind whirred with all the things we'd been through, replaying everything he'd ever said to me. Every look, every touch, every moment we spent together.

I couldn't trust any of it anymore.

"How long, Ryvin? How long were you planning this? When did you suspect I had magic? Was it before or after you kissed me? Did you know I was your mate when we met in Athos? Did you know before you fucked me? Did you know when you told me to kill you?"

"Having regrets?" He asked as he closed the distance between us.

His scent surrounded me, and my breathing grew shallow, my whole body reacting to him despite my anger. My veins were on fire, my skin tingling. My instincts wanted me to claim him in every possible way. I could tell from the way his chest rose and fell, the way his lips parted, the way his eyes darkened, that he was feeling the exact same.

Out of the corner of my eye, I noticed that we had an audience. Dion had opened the door and was leaning against the wall, watching with a smirk on his lips. "Don't stop on my account. This is the most fun I've had in years. I thought you'd be all boring as a human, but darling, that marriage proposal stands."

Ryvin's shadows were around the god in an instant and Dion's eyes widened, bulging as his face turned purple.

"Release him. Now." I marched closer to Ryvin. "Let him go."

The shadows dissipated, and the dark prince glanced at me before turning a glare on Dion. "Don't you dare go near her. We're only here because you owe me a favor, but it didn't include cozying up to Ara."

"You have got to be kidding me. You have no right. I would rather marry him than ever warm your bed again."

Dion laughed, a boyish giggle that filled the room with an effervescent quality. It made me feel light and some of the tension seemed to ease.

"I understand that you don't trust me right now. But don't say things like that. You don't know him like I do." Ryvin glanced toward the god, then looked back at me. "Fuck anyone you want, but please, not him."

"He's only saying that because he knows if you spent some time with me, you wouldn't be able to go back to him." Dion winked.

Ryvin growled, and I held up my hand in a stop symbol before he could take things any further. Turning toward my mate, I caught his stare and, unblinking, held his gaze. "I don't know if I can ever forgive you for what you did. From here on out, I make my own decisions about my life. Understand?"

Ryvin, with the power of two gods, actually looked nervous. He swallowed, then nodded. "Just tell me what you need me to do. Anything."

"I want to finish what we started. My sisters, my kingdom, they aren't safe while the Fae King rules. Or while Nyx is after humans." I held up my hand again, my gesture preventing whatever words were about to escape his parted lips. "And before you say anything, you should know that if you're going to tell me it's too dangerous, and that I can't help, you might want to think twice."

"That's exactly what you were going to say, wasn't it?" Dion said with amusement.

The prince threw a glare at the god but didn't respond.

"No more secrets. No more lies. We work together and we find a way to protect Athos. You owe me at least that." A sudden rush of light-headedness made me stumble and shadows caught me.

I staggered back, away from the swirling tendrils.

"You need to rest. It's going to take you some time to recover," Ryvin said.

"You're all welcome to stay here as long as you need, but if your war follows you to my shores, you're all gone," Dion warned.

I returned to the bed and sat, ignoring the icy chill that sent goosebumps along my arm as Ryvin's shadows slid along my skin. I'd rather it be his shadows than his arms. I wasn't sure I'd be strong enough to stay mad at him if he got too close. "You should leave."

"It is my house," Dion said.

"You can stay, I just want *him* gone," I said, not taking my eyes from Ryvin.

"Darling, I'm not sure you could handle me," Dion said.

"If you touch her…" Ryvin growled.

"Out. Both of you." Laera strolled into the room. "Let her sleep. *Alone.*"

"No. I don't want to sleep." I stood, ignoring the heaviness of my eyes and the increasing throbbing in my temples. "I want to know everything we know. What's going on in Konos? In Athos? Is my family safe? Is the king weakened?"

"You know, your mother would like her," Dion said with a shrug. "Laera's mother, too."

Ryvin's jaw tensed. "None of those problems are going anywhere. You need rest. We can discuss it later."

I shook my head. "No. We discuss it now. I need to know it wasn't all for nothing. Tell me my family is safe, please."

"I'll fill you in, darling," Dion offered. "Anything you want to know."

"That's not necessary." Ryvin extended his hand, and I glanced down, tempted for a moment to accept his offer before looking back up at him without moving. He dropped his arm. "There are clothes in the wardrobe if you want to change."

I glanced down at the thin, nearly transparent nightgown someone had dressed me in, knowing that if I was in a more brightly lit space, I'd be completely exposed.

"Wear whatever you want. There's no rules on my island. And personally, I think you look lovely in what you're wearing," Dion called before walking away. "I'll pour the wine and see you downstairs. Let me know if you want me to banish that mate of yours."

"Don't you dare," Ryvin warned.

A smirk tugged at my lips. "Can he really do that?"

His lips pulled into a tight line, and he nodded.

I hummed. "Good to know. I guess you should be on your best behavior, then."

"I'll see you downstairs." Ryvin closed the door behind him, leaving me in the room alone.

2

ARA

THE HOUSE WAS open and airy. The entire lower floor was surrounded by colonnades that held up the second story. Soft wood floors gave the space a warmth at odds with the opulence of the rest of the formal decor. Plush couches and silk pillows were scattered around in groupings that would allow for conversations.

There were no closed doors, no walls. Just a few well-placed curtains giving the illusion of privacy. Not even a kitchen. Instead, it was like a ballroom and a sitting room collided. It was the perfect party space, which made sense based on the stories. I wondered what this house had seen, then quickly realized I wasn't sure I wanted to know.

Dion was sprawled out on a white couch, a cask of ruby red wine and several glasses on the table before him. Laera sat across from him in a wood chair that didn't look nearly as comfortable as the other furniture. She had the right idea, though. The chairs offered independence. I took the chair next to her and Ryvin settled into the couch on my right.

A woman approached, carrying a tray of food. She wore a white peplos and a crown of flowers atop her long dark hair. With a wide smile, she set it down on the table in front of the god. "For you, my lord."

"Thank you, Adessea." Dion smiled at her, and her cheeks turned pink.

It was an odd exchange, and I watched as she backed out of the room, her head bowed low as she disappeared behind a curtain.

"Don't you tire of all of them begging for your attention?" Laera asked as she plucked a grape from the tray.

"They came all the way here just to serve me," he replied. "I am grateful for all of them."

"After they've abandoned their husbands and children," Ryvin said darkly.

"If their husbands made them feel worthy, they wouldn't be here." Dion poured wine into a glass, then offered it to Laera. "It's my own vintage. None of that fae wine your kingdom is so fond of."

Laera took the cup, then set it in front of her. "I'm not here for ceremony and I am certainly not one of your maenads."

"I don't imagine they'd enjoy your company, Princess," Dion said.

"Clearly there's history here I'm not privy to, but I don't care what it is. I want to know what has been going on since we left Konos," I glanced over at Ryvin. "How did I even get here?"

"The portal," Laera replied.

"It's still active, then?"

Laera nodded. "It's a natural phenomenon at the ley line convergence point. It will be there long after we're all gone."

"Where is Vanth?" I glanced around, half expecting him to join us.

"He is attending to other business," Ryvin said.

"Is he safe?" I asked.

Laera popped another grape into her mouth. "None of us are safe."

"You're safe enough here. My island is a sacred place," Dion said with a grin. "Perhaps Ara will join my maenads. You'll live much longer here with that frail human life of yours than you would if you follow these two."

I threw him a dirty look, and the smile on his face faded. He took a long drink from his glass.

"Perhaps you should stay here," Ryvin said. "Just until we figure out what's going on. Make sure it's safe for you to leave."

"That's not your choice, brother," Laera cut in before I could respond. "Ara is in charge of her own destiny. She's not your concern any longer."

"She's my mate," he hissed.

"Stop talking about me like I'm not here. Laera is right. I make my own choices. Now, is someone going to explain what's going on or am I going to have to find a ship and get off this island on my own?"

"My lord," the woman who'd delivered the food reappeared, lowering her head in submission. "A ship approaches."

I tensed, and Dion's face grew hard and cold. He looked over at Ryvin. "If this is your father's men bringing war to my island, consider our friendship forfeit."

"You two are friends?" Laera asked, her tone amused.

Ryvin lifted a brow but didn't respond.

"Do you think it's your father?" I asked Ryvin.

"White sails," the woman supplied. "Not red."

My shoulders eased a little.

"Well, I suppose we should go and greet our guests," Dion said.

The woman shuddered, then bowed. "I will prepare for visitors."

"You're all coming along, I assume," the god said as he stood. He smoothed out his ivory tunic, then ran his hand through his dark curls. "It's a shame you can't call the monsters anymore. It would be so much easier to take down the ship that way. Though, I suppose *you* could do it, since that magic now lurks in you." He shrugged as he walked past Ryvin.

For a moment, I couldn't breathe. I knew my magic was gone. I knew Ryvin had taken it from me, but it hadn't really sunk in that he could wield it. He really took it all. In addition to the dark shadows he could summon and the death he could command, he could control water and summon monsters. He was already powerful enough before, but the destruction he could cause now was impossible to imagine.

Ryvin set his hand on my elbow, and I flinched, moving away from him. His mouth tightened. "I won't use it; you should know that. I have no intention of ever using your magic."

I moved away from him. "I don't want to talk about this." Dion was already on his way out and I quickly fell into step behind the god, making my way down a wide set of stairs onto a groomed dirt path leading away from the house.

Glowing orbs of light hung in the air along the pathway, illu-minating the darkness of the lush island.

The waiting ship bobbed in the distance, anchored away from the island like a sleeping giant against the starry black-ness. The sea was a void, dark and sinister, only visible due to the moonlight. I hesitated while Dion approached the shore, ready to greet the small boat making its way toward us from the larger vessel. Ryvin glanced my way, but continued forward, following the god to the shore.

"You're afraid," Laera said from behind me.

"I've never been this close to the ocean at night," I explained. There was something else too, an uncomfortable sense of doom that hung over me, making the air itself feel too heavy.

"Your magic probably helped you connect to the sea," Laera suggested. "Now that it's gone, you're going to react differently."

I clenched my hands into fists. The ocean was one of the few things that had always brought me peace. It created a sense of calm, a feeling that all would be right. It was another thing I'd lost. My lower lip trembled as a rush of grief settled inside me. My chest felt tight.

"Don't let him steal that from you. I suspect there's still something left of your mother's gifts. The ocean could still feel like a second home, a place of belonging for you," she said. "They keep saying you're human now, but I don't agree. You're still half-god. There's still some element of that in your blood."

She was right. I couldn't let him take that from me, too. Stepping forward, I walked toward the sand. I reached down to feel for my weapons before realizing I didn't have anything on me. If these visitors were a threat, I wasn't going to be any help. Though, I supposed with Dion and Ryvin, anyone intending to harm us would be destroyed before they could make their first blow.

The incoming boat reached the shore and a single figure stepped out. It looked like a male form, but in the limited light I couldn't see details.

Laera sighed. "I thought we'd left all the wolves behind."

"Vanth?" A flicker of hope fluttered in my chest, and I broke into a run, my feet sinking into the soft sand. I crashed into the shifter, embracing him. "I'm so happy to see you."

He returned the hug. "I'm glad you're safe."

"That's enough," Ryvin growled.

The wolf shifter released me and backed away. "I'm not trying to steal your mate."

"I don't belong to him," I snapped. Were we going to go through this every time I interacted with another male?

Water lapped at my ankles, the sudden cold making me gasp.

"The tide is rising," Laera said.

"Too quickly," Dion added.

Something roared, and my blood ran cold. "What was that?"

"We're not going to stick around to find out," Laera grabbed my hand and tugged me away.

"Did you summon something?" I asked Ryvin as I climbed up the sandy shore toward the rocks.

"That wasn't me," he said. "I told you, I won't tap into your magic. Ever."

My jaw tightened.

"Did someone follow you?" I asked Vanth.

"I don't think so." He glanced over his shoulder.

"Did you get the message out?" Ryvin asked.

"What message?" I looked over my shoulder at the men following behind me.

"So help me, shifter, if you bring this war to my shores..." Dion grumbled.

I almost laughed. He kept threatening, but I wasn't sure he'd actually do anything. I wondered if there was a part of him that wanted the conflict to come here just so he could unleash some of that chaotic magic I'd heard so much about.

"I was able to reach Willarth. He'll get the message to Telos for us," Vanth replied.

"That old coward?" Laera spun, taking my hand with her. I grunted, then pulled away from her grip.

"He's one of the few who isn't in the king's pocket," Vanth said sternly.

"That's because he was cast out," she hissed.

"Reinforcements," Ryvin said. Everyone looked at him, but he was staring at me. "That's what they're talking about. We're requesting reinforcements from the other houses in Telos. The ones we think will be sympathetic to our cause."

"Thank you." I offered a small smile.

"It might not be enough," Vanth added. "The king was surrounded so quickly by his supporters I couldn't get to him. Nobody could. I wasn't the only one who made an attempt to get close enough."

"That's what you did after I went through?" I stared at my friend. "You tried to take him alone?"

"We hoped he'd be weak enough. But no, I didn't attempt. I waited, counting on the help of other silent enemies. I watched them try, all of them failed, so I did what I had to do." He shook his head.

"You had to defend him, didn't you?" I asked.

"We all do things we're not proud of," Laera said. "For what it's worth, shifter, you made the right call. My eyes in the court show that he has more support than we realized."

"He thinks you're still loyal to him?" I asked.

Vanth's jaw tensed, and he nodded. "I'm not sure how long I can get away with being gone."

"Does he know you left?" Ryvin asked.

"I told him I was searching for you," Vanth said. "He's sent every assassin he has after your head. Bounty so high it's going to be impossible to ignore."

"Fuck." Ryvin blew out a long breath. "That was stupid of him."

"It's going to get them all killed," Laera said.

"It's going to bring them here," Dion said through gritted teeth.

"I think you want the chaos," I said, turning to the god. "More dolphins, right?"

He smirked. "War isn't my realm. I'm not allowed to interfere without angering the other gods."

"But you have every right to defend your home," I replied with a shrug.

His lips twisted to the side, and he stared at me for several heartbeats before a smile spread on his lips. "You would have made me a fine wife, you know that?"

"Careful, Dion," Ryvin warned.

"We're done fighting amongst ourselves," Laera scolded. "Nobody is going to ally with us if we can't hold a united front."

"I hate it when you're right," Ryvin said.

"Does that mean Dion is joining us?" Vanth asked.

"I have no idea what you're talking about, shifter. I'm neutral. It's not my fault if you steal my ships or raid my weapons." Dion shrugged, then picked up the pace, walking faster than the rest of us. I almost laughed. I was right, he did want the chaos.

Vanth held out his arm, blocking our progress. We halted while the space between us and Dion widened. Then the shifter turned, his expression deadly serious.

"What is it?" Ryvin asked.

"I watched as six men tried to kill your father. None of them could touch him," Vanth's tone was dark. "They say he's got a protection ward from the sorceress who made the cloud cover. They say he can't be killed."

My heart fell into my stomach. "That's impossible. Everything we did was to weaken him enough so we had a chance."

"We'll figure something out. There's a weakness for all magic," Laera said.

Ryvin's face was an unreadable mask.

"There's more," Vanth added.

We all looked at him, but as soon as his attention shifted to me, I stopped breathing.

"He's planning to attack Athos as soon as the other courts are ready to mobilize their fleets."

Time stopped. It was exactly what I feared, but now it was even worse. It was personal after what I'd done in Konos. The Fae King wasn't going to negotiate. There would never be a Choosing again. There would be only death for every human in my kingdom.

"Let's get to that ship quickly. We have to warn Athos," Ryvin said.

My heart leaped. I wasn't sure I'd ever see my sisters again. It wasn't the reunion I hoped for, but at least I'd get to see my home.

"I always figured I'd die by my father's hand," Laera said. "We might as well get this over with."

3

DION WAS NOWHERE in sight as we set sail on the only ship docked at the island. The crew was nearly silent, only speaking enough to convey anything regarding the sailing of the ship. It was eerie sailing over the endless black of the sea under the stars. A pool of moonlight traveled with us, the reflection in the water the only way to see the churning of the waves.

Closing my eyes, I leaned against the railing, breathing in the salty scent. It used to bring so much comfort, but it came with a twinge of fear now. Or maybe that was regret.

"How are you feeling?"

I opened my eyes to see Ryvin standing next to me. "I'm not sure how I'm supposed to be feeling," I replied.

He looked more polished now. The hour we'd spent preparing to leave had done him good. Even in the dim light of the glowing orbs on the deck, he looked more rested.

Honestly, he looked really good. I swallowed hard, shoving down that part of me that wanted to bury my face in his chest and feel his strong arms wrapped around me.

"I know you're angry with me, but you told me once that you'd trust me," he spoke softly.

"That was before you took my magic."

"You never wanted it. I know you were afraid of it," he replied.

"That doesn't excuse your actions. I was learning how to control it. I was starting to feel like I wasn't weak. You took that from me," I bit out.

"You're anything but weak. We both know that." He reached for me and I pulled away. He retreated, then ran his hand through his hair with a sigh. "I don't regret it. If I had told you, it wouldn't have worked."

"You don't know that," I snapped. "Your research was about a full-blooded goddess and a full fae. I'm not your mother."

"If I thought there was another way, I'd have done it," he said.

"I'm done talking about this with you." My fingers tightened around the railing. "Unless you have something to discuss that has to do with saving Athos, I'd rather we not talk for a while."

He nodded. "If that's what you want."

My chest tightened. It was what I wanted, wasn't it? Then why did I want to run my fingers through his hair and comfort him when he looked at me with that heartbroken expression?

I held my ground while he walked away, finally taking a full breath when he was out of sight. It was impossible to explain the empty void I felt inside. Part of it, where my magic had been; the rest was from missing Ryvin.

Turning from the water, I caught sight of Vanth watching me from his perch on a pile of crates. When we'd first boarded, we'd investigated the boxes and found that they were full of weapons. Dion might not be able to officially help us, but I knew we'd all owe him a favor when this was done.

Vanth lifted his chin, then tilted his head toward the crate on his left in invitation. Silently, I walked over to join him, sitting on the box that I knew contained several dozen well-crafted daggers that were better than anything we'd create ourselves in Athos.

There was something comfortable about sitting with the shifter. We sat for a long while, staring into the darkness, the only sound the occasional murmurs of the quiet crew or the lapping of the waves along the ship as we cut our way toward my home.

"You think we'll be too late when we arrive?" I finally broke the silence but didn't turn to look at my friend.

"The king will need some time to gather his supporters before he attacks," Vanth answered.

"What about Nyx?" I hadn't been able to say it before, but after the promises she made, I was concerned that we'd arrive to find my kingdom decimated by the goddess.

"Ryvin seems to think that her plan is to prevent the sun so the humans suffer."

I glanced skyward, wondering how long we'd be under the dark canopy of night. The lack of sun was going to kill all our crops, which meant all the livestock would perish. No seaweed or fish. Not even the sea would be spared this punishment.

"She always enjoyed the dramatic punishments," Vanth grumbled.

"Was she always so... murderous?" I'd heard the stories, but had she really been responsible for so much damage if she'd been locked away without her powers for so long?

"She can be. Just like all of them." He shook his head. "That's why I tolerate Ryvin. He could have taken another path with his bloodline."

"But you only tolerate him. And I know he fought for his father. But you both hated Laera for her part in the rebellion." I sighed. There was so much history between all of them. "I know it's not my place to ask, but I would like to understand."

Vanth's jaw tensed, and his gaze returned to the sea. I took a deep breath and stared down at my clenched hands in my lap. I knew better than to push someone to speak about things that might be too painful to discuss.

"He was his father's weapon for a long time," Vanth said.

I looked over to find Vanth still staring out at the water.

"My father was the leader of one of the last independent packs. He was instrumental in rallying the others to rebel against the king." Vanth's expression was so far away. As if he was seeing his past play out before him.

I waited, afraid to move, afraid to breathe. I didn't want to startle him or prevent him from continuing.

"I was young. The attack on the castle was my first battle. We knew the power the fae held, but nothing could have prepared us for what the young prince could do. Nobody had seen destruction on that level before. We haven't seen it since. I'm not sure how I survived. Most didn't. I must have been just out of reach. Or the gods decided I needed to watch my father bleed to death before my eyes. I'm not sure why I was chosen to continue on."

I reached over and set my hand on his. He closed his fingers around mine. "I'm so sorry. I shouldn't have asked."

He looked over at me. "It was a long time ago."

"Ryvin killed your father." I let out a breath. No wonder he struggled with his position.

"He also showed up at our home the next day and recruited me to be his personal guard." Vanth's jaw ticked. "I was on the execution list. He spared me."

"Why?" The question came out before I could think better of it.

"I never asked."

"You need to forgive yourself," I said suddenly.

His brow furrowed.

"I might be overstepping, but you accepted a position working for your enemy, for your father's killer. You were young. You wanted to live. You made the right choice," I said.

"Did I?" he asked.

I nodded. "Yes. Because you're here now. And I can't imagine not having you by my side."

"I stood there and watched while they executed those who wouldn't serve the king." He looked away from me, his whole body tense. I squeezed his hand tighter and sat in the silence with him until his shoulders eased.

"We all do things we're not proud of." I had my own list that seemed to grow by the day. "But it's what we do as we move forward."

He grunted, and I got the sense he was finished with this

topic, so I changed it, returning to the present. "Do you think the sun will return?"

"When it does, we'll need to be prepared. Nyx grows her power in the darkness. When the light returns, I think she will as well," he said.

"Well, I guess I'm not in as much of a hurry to see daylight as I thought," I conceded.

Vanth turned so his knees were facing me, and he released my hand. His usual focus had returned, that look he had when he was assessing everything around him. "You should know that the king told Ryvin that if he ended the shifter rebellion, he'd free Nyx and return her powers."

I blinked, taking in the new information.

"Without the destruction your mate wields, we might have had a chance to take down the king before he understood how to use his stolen magic. He knew it, we knew it. We got so close. Ryvin kept his father in power, then learned the truth about him all at once. Even when his father didn't fulfill his promise and release Nyx, it was too late.

"Ryvin was his father's weapon. He had so much blood on his hands, there was nowhere else for him to go. He was despised even more than the king."

My chest felt like it was caving in. So much betrayal, so much loss.

Vanth stood. "We'll be in Athos in a couple of hours. You should try to rest."

I nodded, even though I had no intention of sleeping. My body still ached, and everything still felt so weak, but I was afraid to close my eyes.

Suddenly, the ship pitched, and I was tossed from the crate, landing on my side, only to be thrown rapidly to the opposite side as the ship rocked. Wind whipped my hair into my face and the sea roared. The sky seemed to open, rain pouring suddenly, drenching us in seconds.

The crew was yelling to each other as they moved to new positions, sometimes sliding along the slick deck. I gripped the crate, grateful it had been tied down and rose, only to be knocked down again as the ship rocked violently.

The storm had arrived out of nowhere. Without the sun, it was impossible to see the building storm clouds, but even so, we'd been staring at a starry sky. Had it really changed so rapidly? Goosebumps rose along my arms, but not from the cold. I'd watched so many storms roll in over the ocean. I knew the weather could change quickly over the water, but this felt unnatural.

My tunic and trousers stuck to my body; my hair was plastered against my face. I pushed it aside and peered into the onslaught, trying to figure out where I would be the most help. Probably it was best if I stayed out of the way. I had no idea what I was doing on a ship. The pelting rain stung like ice as it hit my skin and my teeth started to chatter. I needed to get below deck. I was a liability up here.

Carefully, I stood again, bracing myself better this time. Slowly, I turned toward the door that led below and found myself face to face with six figures dressed head to toe in black.

My eyes widened and one of them lunged forward, grabbing me before I could flee.

4

I CLUTCHED at the arm around my throat, digging my fingers into the sopping black fabric of my captor. They didn't even flinch. Twisting and struggling, I tried everything I could to escape, but the hold was too tight for me to break.

"Release her!" Ryvin called over the howling wind.

The arm squeezed tighter around my neck, and I took shallow breaths that were getting harder to come by.

Out of the corner of my eye, I saw the other figures move, closing in around Ryvin. Where was Vanth? Where was Laera? The prince was completely surrounded, though I'd seen him take down more enemies than this without even touching them.

"The bounty is only for you. I don't need the girl," my captor called out in a rough, growling male voice that sounded more animal than human.

I suppressed the urge to shiver, digging my fingernails harder into the arm, hoping to cause pain. "Let me go."

"So brave, this one," he continued. "I can see why you like keeping her around."

"Last warning." Ryvin's tone was deadly.

"Here's the problem. We make more money if we bring you in alive, and we could use the gold." He held a knife out in front of him, showing the blade to Ryvin before placing it against my throat.

I sucked in a breath, then winced when the sharp edge of the blade bit into my skin.

"You kill me, he's just going to make your death more painful," I hissed out.

My captor snarled, then tightened his grip. "No more speaking or I'll end you for the fun of it."

Ryvin moved quickly, attacking the figure standing nearest him with the smooth precision that I had come to expect. The rain continued to pelt, making it harder to see and making the deck slippery. Riven seemed to use that to his advantage, moving even faster by sliding along the planks as he attacked the assassins surrounding him.

I tried to twist free, but each movement caused the knife blade to press harder against my skin. Reluctantly, I stilled, watching as Ryvin fought.

The assassin holding me lowered his lips near my ear and whispered, "I can see why the king prefers to keep him alive. I should have already killed you, but I'm curious to know if your power will return upon his death."

I didn't respond but kept my posture tense, noting that as my captor watched the brawl in front of us, the knife had relaxed enough that it was no longer touching my throat. I blinked away the water droplets that were sticking to my eyelashes, trying to clear my vision, but it was impossible in this deluge. I just needed an opening, I needed a distraction.

Suddenly my captor's arm went limp, falling from my throat, the knife clattering to the ground seconds before his body hit the deck. Quickly, I spun to see Laera grinning at me. She shrugged as if it were no big deal, then ran to join her brother taking down our other foes.

I pushed my hair away from my face, then reached down to grab the fallen man's knife. Before I could decide where to jump into the fray, another set of arms captured me.

"Let me go!" I lashed out, kicking and swinging.

"Calm down," Vanth shouted. "It's just me."

I squirmed in his grip. "Let me go, Vanth."

"So you can get yourself killed out there? I don't think so."

"I still know how to fight," I protested.

"Until you prove that to me, I'm not willing to chance that," he bit out.

Suddenly, Ryvin went down, flat on his back, two of the assassins getting several kicks in before Laera and one of the deck hands grabbed them.

"Ryvin!" I screamed as terror gripped me. He wasn't moving. He was still down. "Let me go, Ryvin needs our help!"

Vanth lifted me off the ground as if I were a child.

"Please, we have to help him!" I tried to wiggle free, but Vanth had me in a tight hold. Ryvin was still on the deck while Laera and the sailors attacked the others.

The shifter carried me while I continued to yell, but I'm not sure he even heard me over the roar of the wind and the patter of raindrops hitting the deck. How could Ryvin be down? I'd seen him take on much greater odds and walk away without a scratch. He even had my magic to aid him now. He should be the most fearsome one out there.

Vanth shoved me into the waiting arms of a sailor I didn't recognize. "Don't let her go."

I struggled as soon as Vanth walked away, turning to face the stranger. "You will release me."

"I don't think so. You can't rip my arms from their sockets," he said.

My jaw tightened. I used to have power that could command that kind of fear. I'd only tasted it for a short time before it was stripped away. I struggled against the stranger's grasp.

"You can try, but if you get away, he's going to kill me," the sailor said.

I stopped moving. He was right, and I didn't want that on my conscience.

Vanth arrived at the fight with a sword in hand. Through the torrent, I could make out his rapid movements as he took on one of the two remaining fighters. Laera was fighting the other and four more littered the deck where Ryvin still lay.

I stopped watching the fight, my eyes locked on the fallen prince. I couldn't tell if he was breathing from here. My whole body tensed, my throat tight. He had to be alright. He had to be alive. I might be furious at him, but I couldn't lose him. I wouldn't lose him.

"Please," I tried changing tactics, "let me go to him. He's injured. Vanth and Laera have it under control. I'll be safe."

"Stop talking." The man tightened his grip, and I fought against the urge to cry from the mounting frustration. I had never felt so helpless before in my life. I couldn't even get myself out of a deckhand's hold. How much of my strength had come from the magic I'd held?

Suddenly, his grip loosened, and I tore my eyes from Ryvin, noting that Laera and Vanth were the only ones standing. I didn't wait before breaking into a run.

Falling to my knees next to Ryvin, I reached for his neck, pressing my fingers to him. There was a faint pulse, but it was hard to find.

"We have to get him below," Laera shouted over the wind.

Vanth was next to me now. He scooped the prince up like a child and carried him, heading toward the trapdoor that led to the belly of the ship. I followed, sparing a single glance back at the remnants of the fight. The crew were dragging the bodies toward the edges of the ship, tossing them into the churning sea.

IT DIDN'T SEEM POSSIBLE. How could Ryvin, with all of his power, be injured? Because he had to just be injured, anything else was completely unacceptable.

I also just knew that if he was dead, I would know. I'd be able to feel it, wouldn't I? It felt like it would be impossible for me to exist in a world where Ryvin wasn't. He had to be alive. There was no other option.

I wasn't sure how I even got down the ladder, but I found myself in the lower deck kneeling next to Vanth. Ryvin was on his back, unmoving.

The interior of the ship was barely lit, and it was difficult to make out his features, but I didn't need light to know every curve of his face. This was my Ryvin.

I still couldn't trust him, and I wasn't sure I would ever forgive him for what he did, but right now, none of that mattered. I pushed his sopping wet hair away from his eyes and ran my hand from his brow down his cheeks. He felt so cold.

"Is he breathing?" Laera asked as she joined us.

"Yes, but he's struggling," I replied.

"He doesn't look good, Laera," Vanth added.

I examined him, moving his soaking wet tunic to try to find any signs of injury. Aside from the grayish tint to his skin, his closed eyes, and labored breathing, I couldn't find anything wrong.

I began working on removing his trousers and his tunic, checking for a wound that needed healing. I must have missed something.

Vanth's hand touched mine, stopping my progress. "He was poisoned. It's the only thing that could take him down."

"That doesn't make any sense. What kind of poison could kill someone like him?" I thought the fae were immune, and he was half-god to add to his strengths.

Vanth held up a small dart. "He had this in his neck when I carried him down."

"What is that?" I stared at the tiny object. How could something so small cause so much harm?

"I didn't know those still existed." Laera took the dart from Vanth. "Who has the resources for this?"

"I'm not sure," Vanth said.

"You're telling me there's a poison that can take down fae and gods?" I asked.

"It's very rare," Laera said. "I thought all who knew how to make it were killed."

"Someone must have saved some," Vanth suggested.

"Or someone learned how and was willing to risk attempting its creation," Laera said, sounding more concerned than I'd ever heard. "I didn't even know there was any ambrosia or fae iron left in our realm to make it."

"It has to be left over from the fae wars. Which means someone might be able to help us," Vanth said.

"What do we do?" I asked, my words coming out far too desperate.

"We need the antidote or he'll die," Vanth replied.

"Where do we get it? And how long do we have?" I knew we needed to change directions. Steer the ship toward wherever we needed to be to find that antidote.

"We need a god. Someone who would be sympathetic to our cause, but they've never welcomed him in their ranks and I can't imagine they would go to any trouble to keep him alive." The set of her jaw and her arms crossed over her chest were the only indication of how frustrated and angry she was. It was the first time I got the sense that Laera did care about her brother, even if the two of them had been largely at odds for a long time.

I closed my hand around the charm resting on my collarbone, then ran my fingers over the cool metal. "What about my mother? Can we reach her in time?" I had never met the goddess, but she had left me behind so that I might live. There had to be some kind of affection there, or at the very least, a desire to see me not die. And right now, with Ryvin struggling for breath in front of me, I felt like I was dying.

"We can't guarantee we'll make it there alive. And I'm not sure this crew will agree to take us there," Laera said.

"Well tell them if they don't, we'll have them all turned

back into dolphins." It was a guess, but considering the fact that Dion's island was completely populated by women, and a ready-made crew had appeared moments before we needed to set sail, I took a guess as to where they had come from.

"Remind me not to cross you when you're mad." Laera turned and climbed up the ladder.

I glanced at Vanth. "Do you think she'll actually help us?"

"I think it's worth a try," he said.

"Do you think he's going to make it?" I asked quietly.

"I'm not sure. But if anyone has a chance at surviving it, it's him. At the risk of bringing up a sensitive subject, the fact that he is full of extra magic might just help. The poison is supposed to eat through the wielder's magic, taking it down bit by bit until there's nothing left, and then it goes after the remaining mortal body. That extra magic he's holding might be enough to save his life."

My breathing was shaky, and for the first time since waking up and learning what Ryvin had done to me, I found that I was grateful for his deception. I'd figure out how to deal with the aftermath, eventually. But I needed him to survive so that there could be a later.

The trap door opened and Laera peered down. "Ara, I need you and that necklace of yours up here. If we run into any of your mother's creatures, we're going to need whatever additional protection we can get."

"On my way," I called.

She vanished from the trapdoor, but left it open.

"Go ahead. I've got it," Vanth said.

I planted a gentle kiss on Ryvin's forehead, then leaned close to his ear. "Don't you dare die on me. I'm not done being angry with you yet."

"You'll get me if anything changes?" I asked.

Vanth nodded. "I'll stay right here until you come back down."

THE RAIN HAD STOPPED and the wind had slowed. It was as if the assassins who attacked us brought the storm with them when they arrived. I wondered if they had. Where had they come from? Magic like that and the poison dart made me think we were dealing with something more dangerous than the Fae King.

Laera was waiting for me on deck. Floating orbs of light hung in the air around her. She turned when she saw me. "The crew is not happy about making this journey."

"Do you have a better idea?" I asked.

"He did steal your magic." she said.

"I won't let him die." Out of the corner of my eye, I caught the faintest smirk on Laera's lips. "Well, let's find out if you have your mother's eyes."

5

Lagina

Of course, there was more to deal with. Because what we'd been through the last few days wasn't enough. So the gods added Sofia's change and my mother's life to their list of ways they were testing me. Or punishing me. And now, the sun was gone. Perhaps the gods themselves were at war. Or maybe someone had killed them all. At this point, I was cheering on whoever could bring them down.

"Should we prepare the soldiers for attack?" Argus asked.

"What soldiers?" Our numbers were so depleted we needed the reinforcements from the wall and the alliance with the dragons to have any hope of even simply protecting ourselves.

"What happened to the sun?" Sophia asked, her voice small and calm. The panicked edge she'd had earlier was gone.

One crisis at a time. That was how I was going to get through this.

"Argus, see that Sophia is cleaned up and cared for. Take only guards you trust with your life. Nobody speaks of this. Understand?"

The guard nodded. "I've got it under control."

"I must go to the temple, ask the gods for guidance," Istvan said.

"No need, old man," a gruff voice called. "I know what's happening."

I turned to see the Dragon King entering the room. My jaw clenched. So much for the guards keeping people away. "Is anyone out there doing their job?"

"I'll take care of it," Argus said, as if reading my annoyance. "Princess, come with me." He extended his hand toward Sophia.

"Go on, Soph," I said.

"Was this the first time?" The Dragon King asked as he scanned the carnage of the room. He didn't even flinch. Didn't seem surprised or bothered by it.

"It was an accident," Sophia supplied.

"The first time is always the worst," the Dragon King said. "She'll feel hungry before she attacks next time. With support, she'll be able to contain it."

My brow furrowed and Argus stopped moving, all of us turning toward the king. "How do you know that?"

"We get the occasional half vampire in Drakous. There are precautions in place, of course, but sometimes, it still ends tragically."

"What happens next, then?" I asked.

"You don't know?" He glanced around the room, then

shook his head. "Your father had himself turned, then never bothered to find out how it might impact his children?"

"I don't need your judgment right now," I snapped. "I'm not my father, but I am the queen of this kingdom."

"I'll take her to her room," Argus said, leading my bloody sister away.

I glanced around the room. "Nobody comes in here until I figure this out, understand?"

"That's a lot of blood to clean," the Dragon King commented.

"Not helpful," I said. "Now, tell me what you meant. What do you know about the sun?"

"I can explain that," Istvan said.

"More secrets, Istvan?" Anger surged. "I thought we were past that."

"Your entire kingdom was built on secrets, your highness," the Dragon King said.

Istvan pressed his lips into a thin line. I could tell he wanted to say something, but it seemed like he was considering his words, which wasn't something he did often.

"Out with it," I demanded.

"We should go somewhere else," he replied, his eyes moving to where my mother lay.

My stomach clenched and suddenly, I could smell the blood and a rush of grief rolled through me, threatening to topple me. It was as if the wall I'd tried to build so I could wade through this crisis crumbled and I was nothing but an orphan who was losing everyone she loved one by one.

A choked sob came from my lips and I blinked away the tears welling in my eyes. Quickly, I wiped them away and forced myself to take a breath and lift my chin. I would have this breakdown privately. Not here. Not now. And certainly not in front of Istvan.

I walked to the doors, knowing the others would follow me. Pausing at the threshold, I found the guard who looked the least green. "See to it that my mother is prepared for a queen's funeral."

The guard bowed. "Of course, your highness."

"Take care with the others. They will also receive services with the highest honors," I added.

"Your highness, the gods dictate..." Istvan began.

I shot him a glare. "They will be honored."

He lowered his head. "As you wish, my queen."

Torches had been lit in the hallways and the few servants I saw wore terrified expressions. Most of them carried bundles under their arms and avoided looking at me. They were fleeing the palace, and I couldn't blame them. If they wanted to go, they had my blessing. It was possible we were at the end, and if they wanted to be with their families, I understood.

As soon as we turned down an empty hall, I turned to the Dragon King. "Explain."

"It's Nyx," he answered.

"The goddess?" My brows furrowed.

"She was in a prison under your kingdom, and my guess is that she got out."

I looked over at Istvan, waiting for the priest to deny the king's claim. He nodded. "That is my guess as well."

"There was a goddess under our city and nobody told me?" That was the last thing I expected to hear. "What else are you hiding from me?"

"You might want to deal with one thing at a time," the Dragon King suggested.

"Call a meeting with the council. I'll meet them in the study shortly." I swept down the hall toward my rooms. I would give myself some time to scream into a pillow and wash my face to hide the tears, then I had work. If we survived long enough, I could mourn my mother once my kingdom was safe.

6

A<small>RA</small>

I <small>COULD PRACTICALLY FEEL</small> the danger lurking around us. With no sunlight, the sparkling blue beauty of the ocean was replaced by an endless black expanse. The moonlight that glimmered on a single patch of the undulating waters taunted us as we chased it closer to where my mother lived.

It was a strange thing charting a course to visit the woman who had left me to grow up with a human father so that I never had any idea that I was different. Part of me was angry at her for leaving me alone all those years, but truthfully, I had never felt alone when I had my sisters with me. Out of place, all the time. Alone, never.

A pod of dolphins swam alongside our ship and I looked at the creatures as their smooth skin caught the glint of the faint moonlight. I wondered if they had always been dolphins or if they were more of Dion's creations. The dolphins vanished suddenly and something else accompanied our ship. A massive creature kept pace with us, occasionally breaking the water so that its scales shimmered with a familiar opalescent sheen. I waited for the fear to come, but it wasn't there. Somehow, I knew the monster wouldn't harm us. Was this the same sea serpent I had encountered in the past, or was this something different?

"We're completely surrounded. Monsters on all sides," a sailor called. "We should turn back. I don't think the goddess wants us here."

"We continue. We've got two on board who wear the protection necessary to get safely through these waters," Laera replied.

My fingers brushed across the serpent charm at my neck, and I hoped it would be enough to get us to the island safely. Just because I felt safe didn't mean we were.

I glanced back at the water and could no longer see the monster, but I knew it was still there. I could feel it.

Extending my fingers, I reached toward the water, trying to call to the power I knew I wouldn't find. When nothing happened, I swallowed hard and pulled my hand back in, balling my fingers into a fist at my side. It was an unnerving feeling. Like something was missing. As if it was just out of reach. I wasn't sure if the glimmer of familiarity I felt was a lingering thread of my magic, or if it was a phantom; a memory of what I once had.

Twice, I called down to Vanth to check on Ryvin. He was still breathing, but that was the only information the shifter gave. I knew that meant things were getting worse. The only reason I stayed on deck was because Laera was convinced I aided our passage. If we were attacked before we made it to the island, there was no hope for Ryvin. So, I waited.

Watching the dark water, listening in to the crew as they argued about how foolish we were to attempt this, and wishing I could beg the gods for Ryvin's life. I knew better than to try to speak to any of them.

DARK CLOUDS BILLOWED IN, sweeping around us and making it difficult to see landfall. "Keep going," Laera instructed, helping guide the ship closer.

We inched closer, blindly sailing in the direction the island had been. I braced myself on the railing, peering into the fog for any signs of danger or land. I couldn't see anything.

Suddenly, the whole ship lurched as we struck land. My body slammed against the railing and I held fast to keep myself upright.

The crew ran around, yelling commands and working quickly to help us debark. I think they wanted to be as far away from the island as possible. I still couldn't see any of them, so I extended my arms in front of me as I walked toward where I thought the entrance to the hold was.

Someone grabbed me and I jumped, letting out a yelp.

"It's me," Laera said. "Vanth already has Ryvin. We have to go. The ship can't stay here. There are too many creatures in the water."

I followed her, trusting that she'd be able to find her way through the thick haze that masked the light of the moon. We didn't walk far before she created an orb of light in her hand, extending it in front of us. The soft gold glow extended just far enough that we could see where our next footfall would land, but anything beyond that was still shrouded.

A shiver ran down my spine the second my feet touched the rocky shore. There was power here, magic I could feel. It set my very bones on edge, making the hairs on the back of my neck rise. The scent of lightning lingered around us, mixing with the brine and salt of the sea. Whatever had caused this fog wasn't natural. It was magic.

Swallowing hard, I silently walked over the rocks toward a shadowy figure. "Vanth?"

"He's still breathing," Vanth responded.

My shoulders eased slightly, but the tension didn't stay away. Every part of me was on alert as we crossed onto soft sand, making our way toward what I hoped was the island and not back into the sea. Each step was a warning, carrying a sense of foreboding that made my skin feel like it had hundreds of tiny spiders crawling all over it. I wanted to leave, I wanted to get back on that ship and head far away. But that wouldn't help us save Ryvin and I could not let him die.

Something wet wrapped around my ankle, halting my progress, and I cried out in surprise. Laera spun, the light illuminating my leg to show a mass of seaweed. Relief made me laugh as I tugged the soggy plant from my skin.

When I looked back up, I could see more. The fog was thinning. Ahead, I saw a dense forest and several figures were emerging from between the trees. I reached for my dagger and cursed when I came up wanting. "I really need to get some weapons."

Laera handed me a knife. "Don't lower your guard. Even if they seem nice."

I gripped the weapon, then moved in front of Vanth. Laera followed.

"What do you think you're doing?" The shifter hissed.

"Protecting your ass," I said.

"You're human, now, remember?"

"I remember. But you have to keep him safe." I hated how I nearly choked on the words, the emotion making my voice thick.

The figures moved closer and Laera sent the light toward them. It floated in the air between us, a circle of gold illuminating the sand and the edges of the trees. The newcomers hesitated, as if afraid to step into the light.

"We're here to see Ceto," I called, unwilling to wait any longer.

"You may pass, but your friends aren't welcome here," a female voice replied. She moved into the circle of light and my jaw fell open in response to her beauty. I had to force my mouth closed. I'd never seen anyone who looked like her. Skin the color of sand, sunshine gold hair, eyes the color of olive leaves. She was stunning. Like spring personified.

Another woman joined her, and she was equally beautiful. With deep green skin and red hair, she was the embodiment of every beautiful flower I'd ever seen. Nymphs. They weren't human. They had to be Nymphs.

"I need her help," I admitted to the creatures. I knew better than to underestimate them. While most of the stories told of them as masters of hiding, I was certain they were capable of far more if they were the welcoming guard for Ceto. "I have to bring him. He's been poisoned."

"Good," a third nymph said as she stepped into the light. Her blue skin shimmered like sparkling water. "The world will be a better place without the carnage he leaves in his wake."

"That's not true," I pleaded. "I need his help. The Fae King is going to attack my people."

"They are not your people, daughter of Ceto," the spring nymph said. "You will live like royalty on this island."

"That's not why I'm here. Please, I have family in Athos."

"Perhaps it's their time?" The blue nymph suggested. "The fates determine what happens to them. Not you."

"That might be true, but I have to try," I added.

"Then go, try." The spring nymph said with a shrug. The three of them turned and headed back toward the woods.

"Wait." I ran after them, abandoning my fear. They paused, turning back toward me, eyebrows raised in silent question.

"I need him. Not for Athos. For myself," I said.

"After what he did to you?" The flower-like nymph asked, not masking the judgment in her tone.

"Your mother will be so disappointed," the blue one added.

"Can I just speak to her?" I asked.

All three pressed their lips into tight lines. I could almost feel their assessment of me. They didn't understand. I wasn't even sure I understood myself. After everything, I still loved Ryvin, even if I wasn't sure if I could ever be with him again. None of that mattered. We might live apart for the rest of our lives, but I needed him to live.

"If any of your friends attempt anything, we will kill all of you. I don't care who your mother is," the spring nymph warned.

"Thank you." I nodded at my friends, and we followed the Nymphs into the woods.

7

ARA

TINY SPARKLES DOTTED the tree line, illuminating a path through the woods. They moved and whirred, flitting around and making everything feel enchanted. It would be a beautiful place to walk and enjoy if the nymphs in front of us weren't a threat.

The path was difficult to see, the way through was overgrown and wild. I wasn't even sure it was a path at all. As we walked, I continued to glance back at Vanth, making sure he wasn't falling behind. He was starting to show signs of struggling with his burden. I could see the sweat glistening on his brow, hear the increased cadence of his breath. How long could he carry Ryvin? I wished I could assist, but I knew better than to offer. I wouldn't be able to support his weight.

"How much farther?" I asked quietly.

"We're nearly there," the nymph in front of me answered.

After a few more steps, they halted, then all of the Nymphs retreated into the trees, vanishing from sight.

"What the fuck?" Laera held her weapon in front of her. "I knew this was a bad idea."

My heart pounded, and I spun in a slow circle taking in our surroundings. Thankfully, the lights continued to glow, illuminating the trees around us, but we were still surrounded by plants. The beach was no longer in view and there was no visible way out. No clear indication of a path.

"They tricked us," Vanth growled. "You can't trust Nymphs."

I felt too hot and too cold all at once. My mind raced, all the worst-case scenarios playing out at rapid fire.

"We have to turn back. Try to find our way to the ship," Laera suggested.

Her words hung like a weight around me, dragging me deeper into despair. We couldn't have come all this way for nothing.

"No." I focused on Ryvin's wilting form. His breathing was so shallow, I could no longer see his chest rise and fall.

Marching forward, I continued in the direction the Nymphs had been taking us.

"Where are you going?" Laera called. "You're going to get yourself killed."

Ignoring her, I shoved the underbrush aside and kept walking. "Ceto! Where are you? Show yourself, you coward!"

Everything I'd bottled up poured out. All my frustration, all my fear, all my anger, all my disappointment and jealousy. All the things I'd felt as that child who never fully fit in.

The heavy weight of my sisters' lives on my shoulders, the responsibility of caring for them while nobody cared for me.

The silent mourning for my mother's loss, the fear that she'd died because of me, the abandonment I felt all over again when I found out she wasn't dead.

"Where are you, *Mother*?" I yelled, hot tears making the back of my eyes sting.

"Ara, turn around," Vanth hissed.

"Are you hiding? You just abandon me, then run away?" I wasn't even sure what I was saying anymore, but I kept yelling. Kept calling out to the goddess who had birthed me. The mother who abandoned me.

A gust of wind made all the trees shake, and the flickering lights went out. Laera grabbed my arm and tugged. "Ara, we have to go."

I pulled away from her and continued walking in the dark, stumbling over branches and vines, picking myself up after I fell, only to fall again.

"Are you even here? Are you happy with yourself? Happy with what became of me? Happy that your power is gone from my veins so you no longer have to claim me?" I picked up my pace, blindly charging into the trees. I was lost, overwhelmed and terrified and angry and heartbroken. All the feelings swirled into a cocktail of madness, making it impossible to settle on one emotion.

What did any of it matter? What if I angered a goddess? I was starting to wonder what else I could lose. What else I would even be allowed to keep. I had opened my heart to Ryvin, and he'd betrayed me. Yet, he was mine. I still wanted him. I didn't want to lose him.

I emerged into a clearing, halting as soon as I saw the moonlit open space. An unassuming house filled my view, complete with a massive bonfire burning in front of it. Smoke

billowed up, rising toward the stars. The warm glow illumi-
nated the space, casting writhing shadows on the gathered
creatures. Several appeared almost human, possibly more
Nymphs. Some had horns or tails, others appeared more
plant than person.

Each of them turned, their eyes watching me with curious
expressions. None of them left their place around the fire. For
a moment, I stood there, frozen, wondering if I was in the
wrong place.

But I could feel it. I knew Ceto was here. I knew my
mother was here. The same way I knew the entire island was
dripping with magic.

"Where is she?" I asked, my voice steadier this time.
"Where is Ceto?"

"Did you come all this way to lash out at me for abandoning you?" A refined, dignified feminine voice asked. A
woman emerged from the opposite side of the fire, her movements graceful and flowing, reminiscent of the way the water
serpent moved through the sea.

"Mother?" It was question and statement. Acknowledg-
ment and condemnation.

We stared at each other for what felt like hours, but I
knew it was only a few heartbeats before her head snapped to
the side, taking in my friends as they approached.

"He is not welcome here," she said. "None of them are
welcome here."

"They are with me. And we need your help," I admitted.

A feline smile spread on her lips. "You come here, with
your anger, seeking my assistance?"

"I do," I agreed.

"He succeeded, I see. Your magic is gone," she observed.

I nodded, not bothering to let myself linger on the fact that she knew what he was going to do and that she'd done nothing to stop it. If anything, that meant she was in on the betrayal. It should have hurt more than it did, but there wasn't a whole lot that hurt more than being led to believe she was dead all my life.

"He was poisoned," I said. "I need to know if you have the antidote."

She frowned and appeared to be contemplating my words.

"Can you help us?" I asked.

Vanth stepped forward, pausing next to me, Ryvin still in his arms. "He's almost out of time."

"I'm not sure how that's my concern," Ceto said.

"Because when he dies, her magic returns," Laera said.

I tensed, my head turning to face the princess. I hadn't even considered that. Something deep within, a dark, slithering thing reared its head, rejoicing at the prospect of returning that stolen part of me. Almost as quickly as it rose, I stifled it, sending the wistful darkness away. I would not regain my magic from Ryvin's death. Another part of me, the part that was tied to him was screaming in pain. That part of me knew we were so close to losing him forever.

"They'll come for her if she has her magic," Vanth added.

I hated that we were leveraging this. I hated what Ryvin had done. I hated that my magic was gone, but they were right. The gods would come for me. Here. On Ceto's island.

"Can you save him?" I asked.

"I suspect it was the final death," Vanth supplied.

Ceto's brows lifted. "That's a rare poison."

"It's the only thing that could do this to him," Vanth said.

"Please, is there anything you can do?" I asked, my tone just shy of begging.

We'd gathered an audience. Several female figures fanned out around the goddess, watching with interested expressions. Their nearly human features were cast in sharp relief by the dancing shadows of the bonfire, making them take on ghostly masks that reminded me that none of them were human. And that all of them could probably kill me without thinking twice, even if they appeared as delicate as the flowers they resembled.

"Mating bonds are such a curse," she said with a sigh. "Come along."

We followed her toward the house. The exterior was simple. Stucco walls with a tile roof. The kind of house I'd expect to see a merchant living in. Not a goddess. It was nothing like Dion's sprawling marble home.

The interior told a different story. It was much larger inside than I anticipated. Gleaming polished floors, exquisite furniture, beautiful sculptures... any simplicity the exterior promised melted away.

We passed a colorful marble statue of three women dancing together, their bodies surrounded by flowers. For someone who was considered the goddess of monsters, I was surprised at the connections to nature. Aside from the nymphs, the walls of her home were covered in frescoes and mosaics of flowers and plants. I wondered if a different goddess had once called this place home.

"Put him here," Ceto instructed, pointing to a long ivory couch. Vanth lowered the incapacitated prince to the cushions, then stepped back. He shook out his arms and rubbed his shoulders.

"Thank you for carrying him," I said.

He nodded, then walked away, still rubbing at his shoulders.

"Can you do it?" Laera asked. "Do you have the antidote?"

"I do, but I'm not sure if it's going to work." She leaned down and pressed her fingers to his neck. She frowned, then looked up at me. "He's almost gone. You do realize, if it's his time, nothing can reverse that."

"It can't be his time," I said. "Not yet. I'm not done fighting with him."

"I can respect that," Ceto almost smiled. "But it's not enough of a reason to use my last vial of the antidote."

"Please, if there's a chance..." my voice was shaky, the fear of losing him replacing the anger I'd been channeling only moments ago.

"You'd allow him to live after what he did?" she questioned.

"I can't lose him. I know it doesn't make sense, but I need him alive," I said.

She sighed, then stood. "I'll be right back."

"Thank you," I said.

With a nod, she turned and left the room.

Laera and I both stared down at the man on the couch in front of us. He'd never looked so fragile before. "What if it doesn't work?" It seemed dangerous to even say those words out loud, but I knew she had to be thinking the same thing.

"Then we'll have to figure out how to keep the gods from killing you," Laera replied.

"Am I making a mistake?" I asked.

"For what? For not letting him die? For trying to save him? For still being in love with him, even though he betrayed you?" She looked over at me, one brow raised, waiting for me to respond.

I shrugged. All of it. None of it.

Ceto swept back into the room, her long sheer gray peplos dragging on the shining tan floor. She held out a bottle in front of her. "This bottle has been sitting here for longer than he's even been alive, but it's the only dose I have."

"I appreciate you doing this for him," I said.

She clicked her tongue. "I'm not doing this for him. If it were up to me, I'd watch him take his last breath. He deserves it for what he did to you. And honestly, I've killed people for far less."

"I know."

"I'm not even doing this because you love him. You'll learn that a mating bond doesn't mean you're stuck with him." She knelt down next to him, holding the bottle over his face. "I'm doing this because if your magic returns and you're not prepared, everything I did to keep you alive will be for nothing."

"So you agree with him? You approve of what he did?" Laera asked.

"Not at all. One day, I'd like to see her slay him herself. Reclaim what he stole." She looked over at me. "When you're ready to face the gods so you can prove you're worthy of my power, of course."

I tensed, my mind considering it for a single heartbeat. Claiming my magic made that dark part of me ignite. But it was quickly extinguished. I could never do what she suggested. "Why me?" I turned it around, knowing that all the gods had multiple illegitimate children. "Why did you hide me from them?"

"Because I fell in love," she said.

"Gods fall in love with mortals all the time," I pointed out.

She tipped the contents of the bottle into Ryvin's mouth, then stood. With a knowing smirk, she chuckled. "That's true. But the day you were born, I had a visit from Nona, and she said you had no future. No path. She told me you were too dangerous to allow to live so I hid you away, knowing that one day, you were meant to challenge the gods. And when that day comes for you to reclaim your magic, I'm going to laugh as you burn it all."

I wouldn't have believed a word Ceto said if Morta hadn't said something similar. But I knew better. I'd never harm Ryvin. I hated how much I still felt for him after everything, but those feelings would fade over time. I could learn to live without my magic, even if I never forgave him for taking it.

"How long till we know if it worked?" I was done asking personal questions that I wasn't ready to deal with.

"I'm not sure. I haven't seen it used in a long while. I imagine if he's still breathing in the next few hours, you've got a good chance that he'll survive."

Ceto rose, then stood in front of me, her eyes scanning me, taking me in from head to toe. I held my breath under her inspection, unsure how to respond. She was my mother, but there wasn't any connection there, no tenderness.

"You're welcome to stay here after he leaves. The fae are going to destroy everything," Ceto warned.

"You know I can't stay," I replied.

"I know. But I'm still your mother," she replied, offering a weak smile. She brushed her fingers over the charm at my throat. "This will allow you to return if you ever change your mind."

I nodded. "Thank you."

Ceto, my mother, turned abruptly. "Marina, please show them where they can rest while they wait on the prince."

A nymph with pale green skin and dark blue hair stepped forward. I had no idea how long she'd been standing there. She inclined her head, then gestured for us to follow.

Vanth wordlessly appeared next to Ryvin, lifting him once more. I knew he hated having to carry the prince, and I wondered if he'd have let him die if not for me.

We were shown several rooms to choose from. I selected a room with a chair next to the bed so I could sit with Ryvin.

"You should get some sleep," Vanth suggested.

"I will." I wanted to stay awake and monitor him, but I knew my body would eventually drag me under. At least I'd be in the chair near Ryvin, though. It wouldn't be a deep sleep that way and I'd be alerted to any movement.

"Think we can trust them not to kill us while we sleep?" Laera asked quietly.

"I'm pretty sure if she wanted us dead, we'd already be in the deep," Vanth said.

Laera hummed but didn't argue as she left the room.

"I'm right next door if you need anything," Vanth said as he lingered in the doorway.

"Thank you for all you did for him." My words weren't enough to show my gratitude. "I know how complicated things are between the two of you."

"If I hadn't carried him, you'd have tried to do it yourself," he replied.

He had a point.

"I can't say I approve of what he did, but I am glad you're still alive." Vanth nodded, then grabbed the doorknob. "Try to sleep."

"See you in the morning," I responded out of habit. What even was morning anymore? We hadn't seen the sun since we left Konos.

He grunted a response, probably thinking the same thing, then closed the door. Leaving me alone with the still unconscious prince.

8

ARA

THE SOUND of dripping water echoed through the cavern. I reached out, feeling the rough stone under my fingers, desperate to find the way out. Somewhere ahead, there was light, and I carefully crossed the uneven ground, my feet slipping on pebbles as I walked. With each step, the light seemed to dim, getting farther with every passing breath.

I wasn't sure where I was going, but I knew I had to make it to that light. Picking up my pace, I moved faster, dragging my fingers along the wall at my side for balance.

"Ara?"

The voice was familiar, but new all at once. I wasn't sure who it was, but I knew it was important. "Cora? Is that you?"

"Ara, hurry!"

I moved faster, nearly falling more than once, but somehow managing to stay upright. "Sophia?"

"Please, Ara, I need you."

My heart raced and tension coiled inside me like a snake waiting to strike. I had to get to whoever was calling for me. It was life or death. I didn't know who it was or where I was, but I knew that much.

"Hold on!" I yelled, catching myself as my ankle rolled on a loose stone. The light was fading. I was running out of time.

Releasing the wall, I raced forward, giving everything I had to dash through the cave. I had to get there before it was too late. That light couldn't fade, I couldn't lose it.

Finally, I emerged into the glow and shielded my eyes from the intensity. "Hello?" I called, squinting into the light. I was no longer in the cave. The sun glowed warmly above me and I tipped my head back, eyes closed, feeling the warmth on my face, reveling in the sensation. I could smell the sea, hear the rustling of the wind in the trees.

All the fear and concern I'd felt seconds ago melted away. I opened my eyes and looked around, taking in my new surroundings. I was standing in a field of red poppies and ahead was an unfamiliar structure. Four columns framed a square platform, billowing blue fabric suspended between them, acting as a roof. In the center of the platform were two gorgeous white couches, deep blue pillows strewn across them. It was an inviting space.

Slowly, I walked toward it, knowing I was supposed to go there. This was where I'd been called to. But where was the person who'd been calling me? Hadn't there been something dangerous or desperate happening? This was peaceful, calm, happy.

The couch was just as soft and inviting as it appeared and I sat, pulling one of the pillows into my lap, giving it a squeeze. What had I been worried about? Everything was just fine.

"Ara?"

That voice I knew. I'd know that voice anywhere. I was on my feet in a heartbeat, the pillow abandoned. "Ryvin. You're alright."

His brow furrowed. "Of course I'm alright." He was dressed differently. His usual black replaced by a soft blue tunic, the color of Athos. Of home.

He stepped onto the platform and my breath caught as I stared at him. I'd forgotten how handsome he was. How his eyes pulled me into their silver depths, how I could stare at his lips for hours, how I wanted to touch every inch of him just to remember how he felt.

Ryvin paused in front of me. "We haven't had enough time alone lately."

That seemed true, even if there was a strange nagging sensation tugging at me, almost warning me. His large hands settled on my hips, and he moved closer until my chest was against him.

A flicker of discomfort rose and I took a step back, wondering why I was struggling to connect with him. How could that be? Was it because of the voice earlier? I glanced around, half expecting to find someone watching us.

"Is everything alright?" he asked.

I turned back to him, wondering why I was feeling so conflicted. Ryvin was everything I wanted.

He gently caressed my arm, the touch soothing. "Should we go home?"

Home. My brow furrowed. Home. With Ryvin. Wasn't that what I wanted? Was that what we had? "Where is home?"

He brushed his thumb over my lower lip. "Home is wherever you and I are together, you know that."

I did, didn't I? It made sense. He was home. When I was with him, I felt like I belonged. I closed my eyes, leaning into his touch as his thumb caressed my jaw, then my cheek. His hand moved to the back of my head, his fingers threading into my hair. When he gently pulled me closer, I didn't resist.

As soon as his lips met mine, my mind emptied. The only thing I could think about was him and me.

His hands were everywhere all at once, touching, caressing, squeezing. I moaned into his kiss, relishing the sensations dancing across my sensitive skin. He tasted like honey and wine and salt, and I needed more of him. I returned his kiss with eagerness, our movements working in a tandem frenzy. My hands slid around his broad shoulders and I gripped him tighter, my fingers digging into his back.

He groaned and the sound was like a pulse of need, making my insides molten. His hand moved to my throat, and he tilted my chin back with his thumb. I whimpered as the kiss was interrupted, but before I could complain, his teeth were on my lower lip, biting just hard enough to introduce pain before he sucked it into his mouth. One hand was on my back, the other under my peplos, caressing my breasts. He expertly played with my nipples, touching and pinching, making me suck in little breaths as pain and pleasure combined.

When his mouth claimed mine again, I went boneless, falling into his waiting arms. He lowered me onto soft cushions. Had those been there before? My mind was too fuzzy. It didn't matter. The only thing that mattered was that he was here with me.

I slid my hands under his tunic and ran my hands over his warm skin, feeling all the hard muscles under my fingers. He pulled the fabric over his head and discarded it. My hands stilled, and I took a moment to devour him with my eyes. I'd forgotten just how incredible every bit of him was. His broad chest was firm and strong, leading down to a muscular stomach and well-defined vee at his hips. I bit down on my lower lip as I moved to the waistband of his trousers.

He grabbed my wrists, then lowered himself on top of me, keeping my arms pinned above my head. His lips trailed kisses along my jaw and down my neck before moving to my collarbone.

My wrists were free now and while he gathered the fabric of my peplos, pulling it up around my waist, I worked on his trousers, using my thumbs to lower them.

He nipped at my neck, then slid his arm behind me so he could lift me. My dress was off in a flash, and he kicked his trousers aside. We were gloriously, deliciously naked and the moment his body pressed against mine I gasped as tingles danced along every bit of my skin. It was like little bursts of lightning making me feel more alive than ever before.

His mouth was on a nipple, sucking and teasing. I wrapped my legs around his waist, pulling him toward my center. My hands slid along his bare back, moving lower until I reached his ass. I urged him closer, my breathing coming out in desperate pants. "I need you inside me."

"I love it when you beg," he said.

I could feel his hardness at my entrance. He brushed against the sensitive skin and my breathing hitched in anticipation. "Stop teasing me."

He growled, then playfully nipped my breast while his

hand teased the other. I dug my fingernails into his back, my eyes closing as I oscillated between the pleasure of the sensations and the frustration of not feeling him inside me.

Just as I'd let my guard down, he slammed into me. My back arched and I cried out, gripping the cushions under me for support. He grabbed my legs, lifting my hips as he continued to thrust. I gasped as he reached a place inside that made me moan and gasp, crying out over and over. I was so close, the pleasure building so much I held my breath. The pressure intensified, my insides feeling as tight as a spring. Finally, it broke, releasing like a tidal wave. My body shuddered and stars exploded in my vision. I cried out, grabbing hold of Ryvin and pulling him close to me.

He groaned, shaking as he found his own release. Leaning down, he pressed his forehead against mine. We were both damp with sweat and panting. I pushed hair away from his eyes, then pressed my hand to his cheek. He smiled softly, a smile of pure joy. It was so genuine and intimate that I melted, my whole body relaxing into the feeling of the two of us. I could die happy if it meant seeing him smile like that.

He situated himself next to me, pulling me over so I was resting on his chest. "The stars are beautiful tonight."

I looked up, seeing the sparkling lights through the breaks in the billowing canopy. A cool breeze made goosebumps rise on my damp skin. "I don't want to go."

"I know." He kissed my forehead and I closed my eyes, leaning into the feel of his lips against my skin.

"Why can't it be like this all the time?" I asked.

"Because life is a tragedy," he replied.

9

ARA

"ARA?" The scratchy voice woke me with a jolt, the lingering memory of the dream making my cheeks flush.

"Ara? Where are we?" Ryvin asked.

"You're awake." I jumped from the chair and leaned over him, trying to make out his appearance in the faint glowing light. All embarrassment from the all too real dream faded, replaced by the relief of seeing him alive. "How are you feeling?"

He grunted as he sat. "Like I was chewed up and spit back out. What happened? Where are we?" His forehead creased as he looked around the room.

"You were poisoned. We nearly lost you," I explained.

He rubbed his forehead, then the back of his neck. The grimace on his face told me he was still feeling the effects of the poison. At least he was awake. That had to be a good sign.

"There's not a whole lot that can take me down," he said after a long pause.

"It was something rare. Vanth thinks it was the final death."

"I didn't even think there was anyone who could make that anymore." He stretched out his arms, then braced himself on the bed before standing.

I rose to my feet and reached to steady him. "Careful."

"I'm alright," he assured me, placing his hand on top of mine. "I'm already feeling better. Where did you get the antidote?"

I'd tried avoiding telling him where we were, but he'd find out as soon as we left the room. And the quicker we got off this island to head to Athos, the better. "We're on Ceto's island. It was the only place we could think of that might have the antidote."

His brows lifted. "And she gave it to you? For me?"

"I suspect it was for me," I admitted. "She said if you died, I'd get my magic back."

"That makes more sense," he replied. "Your mother doesn't exactly care for me."

"All the more reason for us to get out of here. You think you can travel?" I wasn't sure how long we'd been here, but I was feeling more rested than I had in months.

"Where's everyone else?" he asked.

"They found rooms to rest in while we waited for you." I placed my hand on his lower back, worried he needed the support.

He didn't push me away as we made our way to the door. The two of us moved in silent agreement from the room. It didn't take long to find the others sitting on the fancy white couches around a low marble table. Vanth stood as soon as he saw us, the shifter almost smiling at the sight of Ryvin. "You pulled through."

"Sorry to disappoint you," Ryvin said, almost playfully.

I glanced out the windows, noting that it was still dark. "How long were we asleep?" I asked.

"It's been a day already," Laera said. "And we have news."

Ryvin and I made our way over to the couches. We appeared to be the only ones in the home. "Where's Ceto?"

"I don't think she likes spending time around us," Laera said with a shrug. She pushed a plate of olives and cheese and a basket of flat bread toward us. "Eat."

My stomach growled and I picked up an olive.

"What's the news?" Ryvin asked.

"Nyx is indeed sleeping. Ceto agrees that we'll know when she's awake when the sun returns," Laera explained.

"Well, at least that's one less thing we have to worry about at the moment." Aside from the fact that without the sun, we had a lot of other problems, but I wasn't sure which was worse. A goddess seeking vengeance, or a lack of crops and sunshine. One problem at a time.

"We also found out that the Fae King has gained a formal alliance with the vampires in Thebes, as well as the Court of Vipers, and the Court of Thunder," she said.

"That's disappointing," Ryvin said.

"The vampires from Thebes are ruthless and mindless. It's a mistake for him to ally with them. They'd turn on him just for fun. Having them around is risky for all of us," Vanth said.

"I thought your mother hated him. Does her court really want to join or is it because she's tied to him?" I asked.

"She'll support him unless we weaken him enough for her to change sides. She's only loyal to herself," Laera replied.

"What about the others you were trying to reach?" I asked. "Didn't you say you had someone trying to get some people on our side?"

"I thought we'd lock down the Court of Thunder. Them joining the king is a blow," Vanth said.

"We still have some options," Ryvin added. "No word from the Gold Court or the Mountain Dwellers?"

"Not yet, but I wouldn't count on the Mountain Dwellers to break their independence for this," Vanth said.

"They won't maintain it for long if my father succeeds in eliminating the Dragon kingdom," Ryvin said.

"Do you think that's even possible? You said he's never held it before and now he's weaker than he was." I reached for a piece of bread, then added some of the cheese before folding it.

"They can't shift in Athos," Ryvin said.

"What?" That was news.

"There's not enough magic there for them. It takes a lot more to turn into a dragon than it does to turn into a wolf," he explained. "When I was there, it was restricted. It took a lot more to make my magic work, and I was limited on how often and how much I could use. I only got through it because of my mother's blood. If he attacks while they're still in Athos, he might have a chance to weaken them."

I set down the bread without taking a bite. "We have to go. Now. We have to warn them."

"I already summoned the ship," Ceto said as she walked into the room. Her eyes found Ryvin. "You survived, I see."

"Is anyone happy you're still alive?" Laera asked, her tone dripping with sarcasm.

Ryvin glared at her, and I stifled a giggle.

"Now, you three out. I want a word with my daughter," Ceto declared.

It was as if all the air was sucked from the room. Ryvin moved closer to me, his arm touching mine.

"It's fine," I assured him. "Go on, I'll be right there."

Vanth stood, then cleared his throat. "Thank you for the hospitality." He inclined his head in the most respectful gesture I'd seen from him.

Ceto inspected him briefly, then made a dismissive gesture with her hand. He quickly retreated, heading toward the door.

Laera bowed. "Lovely to see you, as always."

"If you harm her..." Ryvin started.

I elbowed him. "Don't start. I've got this."

"Out, princeling," Ceto commanded.

He pressed his lips into an annoyed line, but he exited behind his sister. Ceto gestured to the couch, and I sat. She took the seat across from me, the table between us. She waved her hand and two glasses of wine appeared. My lips parted and my eyes widened.

"I can't make the wine, but getting it to appear is a cute trick. It's magic you probably could have wielded with some practice, since wine is just another form of water when you really think about it." She picked up a glass and took a long drink, then set it down. She inclined her head toward my glass, clearly indicating that I should drink.

My stomach twisted. Was this a test? I didn't think she'd harm me. After all, she could have easily done so already. I brushed my fingers over the charm at my neck, a reminder of the fact that despite abandoning me, she'd sent someone to deliver a way to help me stay safe while crossing the sea.

I lifted my glass and took a sip. It was sweet and delicious. I set the glass down, waiting to see if anything happened.

"I can't say I agree with your choice of companions," Ceto began, taking another drink of her wine, "but I am impressed by the fact that you're still alive."

Were we having a heart-to-heart? "Um, thank you."

"You're meant for something great; I know that. I just didn't think this was your path. So if you ever decide that you're not where you should be, you're welcome to return here," she offered.

The door opened and Vanth peeked inside. "The ship is ready. I'll wait for you outside."

Ceto picked up her wineglass. "You should go. Try to live a bit longer. I think I'm getting the hang of this whole motherhood thing."

I stood. "Thanks for letting us stay here. And for helping Ryvin."

"One last thing." Ceto crossed to me and extended the hand that wasn't holding the wineglass, showing a small leather pouch. "Don't open it until it's absolutely necessary."

"What is it?" I asked.

"I can't tell you that," she replied, passing the pouch into my hand. "But it's vital you keep it sealed until you need it."

"Then how will I know?" I asked.

"You just will." She walked to the door and opened it. "Now, go. Next time I see you, the world will be a different place."

10

CORA

"WHAT IS GOING ON?" I demanded as soon as I threw open the door.

The Dragon King wasn't in his bedroom, but his men had been stationed outside the door. Maybe that's why they hadn't stopped me from entering.

"Well, this is a nice surprise," his deep voice said as he rounded the corner from the bathing chamber. His long red hair was slicked back and still wet, and he was in the process of drying himself without concern about covering anything.

He rubbed the towel over his strong shoulders and muscular chest before drying his stomach. My eyes worked their way down his body, taking in the defined muscles of his stomach to the divot at his hips, pointing my attention lower. The towel was behind him now, leaving everything on full display. Heat built low in my belly and I clenched my thighs against the tingling sensation between my legs. I lingered at his impressive cock before I realized what I was doing. Cheeks heating, I clenched my jaw and reminded myself that I was not supposed to find this man attractive. I was still trying to figure out a way to get out of this marriage.

When I met his eyes, he was smirking. "I'm glad you like what you see. That will make our wedding night more enjoyable for both of us."

"It's adorable how you still think I'm going to marry you," I snapped.

"You did eagerly enter my room and then proceed to devour me with your eyes." He shrugged.

"I did not devour—you know what? That doesn't matter. I'm here because my sister won't tell me what is happening, but apparently you've been in meetings with her all day. Or night, whatever the fuck this is, since the sun decided to not return." I crossed my arms over my chest and made myself keep my attention on his face.

"It is not my place to share what the queen might not want her subjects to know."

I scoffed. "Her subjects? I'm her sister."

"You are not the ruler, though. Sometimes a ruler must keep things from others for the good of the kingdom," he said.

I moved closer to him, my jaw sore from how hard I was clenching. "I don't know how you do things in Drakous, but I refuse to sit by and watch passively. That didn't work so well for Ara, and I know my mother would never allow such an insult."

"Your mother is dead," he said.

Ice ran through my veins and I took a step back, trying to reframe the words he'd just said. I must have heard him incorrectly; there had to be another explanation. Maybe it was a translation issue. I knew they spoke common in Drakous, but they had their own language, too.

"I'm sorry. I imagine your sister will tell you when she's ready. Consider this my peace offering. Showing you I will work to be a decent husband to you by treating you as an equal."

My brows lifted. "Peace offering? Telling me my mother is dead? And decent? Who wants a decent husband? I wanted love and devotion and late nights under the stars and lazy mornings in bed. I wanted children and warmth and affection. None of which you can provide."

"For a princess, you had an incredibly unrealistic idea of what marriage would be. Royals don't get to choose." His expression was almost pitying.

"Don't give me that look. I grew up in the only human kingdom and I'm not heir to the throne. As far as I knew, I'd marry a wealthy merchant, which Tomas was. Well, he would have been when his father retired." Shame and disappointment made my cheeks heat. I thought I'd found someone to spend my life with and I hated the idea that I'd made such a huge mistake.

"He didn't deserve you," he said gently.

"Don't give me that. I don't want your pity. Of course, he turned me down when faced with you. Have you seen yourself? You're terrifying. You could probably tear off his arms and that's in your human form..." I stopped myself, unable to continue as reality slammed into me. He was dangerous enough as he was, but he could get worse. There were times when he was a true monster. A creature with scales and wings who could breathe fire. And I was expected to bed him?

I think not.

"If that's what you need to tell yourself." He shrugged.

I wanted to slap him, but I reconciled myself with the fact that I'd rather see him smug than feeling sorry for me. "What happened to my mother?" I changed the subject, done thinking about the impossible situation of being married to this man.

"I think it's better if the queen tells you."

"What happened to being decent? It's not going to change the fact that she's dead, is it?" My throat tightened, and I fought to hide my emotions. I would not give this stranger the satisfaction of seeing me with any form of weakness. If my mother really was dead, it's the least that I owed her.

She'd want me to maintain control. Especially over a man. It was what she'd trained me for. All those private lessons, just the two of us, where I learned how to bat my lashes and smile coyly. How I'd learned to show just the right amount of skin to draw attention. Of course, she'd regretted that later when I took her teachings and ran with them. She thought she could control me, but she gave me just enough information to find my own power. And my own pleasure.

I stared the king down, silently waiting for him to crack. If I was stuck with him for the time being, I would have to find a way to get what I wanted from him and right now, it was information.

"What happened?" I pressed.

"Sophia," he replied.

I tensed. "Explain."

He shook his head and his shoulders sunk. If I didn't

know better, I'd say he was genuinely uncomfortable sharing bad news with me. I took a step closer to him and softened my tone, knowing I might have pushed too far. "Please."

His eyes caught mine. "Your younger sister is half-vampire. It seems nobody knew. When they have their first craving for blood, they take it from anyone they can. Your mother was in the wrong place at the wrong time."

My knees gave out, but I didn't hit the floor.

"I got you." The Dragon King held me, preventing me from falling. "I'm sorry you had to find out like this."

Remembering myself, I pushed away from him and smoothed out the wrinkles in my peplos, keeping my eyes on the floor so he couldn't see me blinking away the tears. After a few sniffles and deep breaths, I collected myself. "Thank you for telling me. That wasn't so hard, was it?"

"You don't have to pretend it doesn't bother you. I respect a strong woman, but you're allowed to feel things," he said.

"I don't owe you my feelings," I snapped.

"If that's how you want things to be." He didn't hide his irritation.

I didn't want to talk about my mother or my sister. Was Sophia even alive? Did they kill her for what she did? For what she was? I shoved the thought away, focusing on the other pressing issue. "Why is it dark?"

"Nyx is angry," he said simply.

I arched a brow. I wasn't even sure I believed that the gods were actually out there somewhere. "Nyx? The goddess? She hasn't interfered in our world in generations. Why would she suddenly reappear?"

"Probably because Athos was hiding her prison."

I placed my hand on my forehead, then lowered it as I shook my head. "Athos did what?"

"I think you should talk to your sister about the rest of this," he said.

"You'll tell me. If you want any chance at getting in my bed, you're going to make it worth my while," I snapped, surprised at myself for the words. Too late to call them back.

He almost looked like he was going to laugh, then he pulled himself together. "Does that mean you're entertaining the idea of me and you in bed together?"

"Just answer my questions," I replied.

He moved so close I caught the scent of leather and spices, hating that I actually liked the way he smelled. His voice was low, and his lips were near my ear. "The Fae King kept her locked up below your city. It's why he never touched Athos. It's why we never came for Athos, even though your people were so hungry for our blood."

My pulse raced and my first instinct was to deny him, but explained why the fae hadn't just wiped us out long ago. "How did she get out?"

He took a step back and his absence made me feel suddenly cold. I had to resist the urge to move closer to him.

"That's the part we don't know," he admitted.

11

ARA

EMPTY SHIPS BOBBED in the harbor, fishermen's nets lay abandoned. There were no lights to greet us, just darkness. "Looks like we're the only ones sailing here now," I commented.

"I'm guessing those are the temples?" Laera asked, pointing toward the beacons of light glowing on the hillside in front of us. The parts of the city I could see over the walls were just as dark as the shore, but the temples scattered throughout were lit up as if it were a feast day. Smoke billowed from them, and I knew they were making offerings that would fall on deaf ears.

"They must all be gathered at them," I said. "But they're praying to the wrong gods. There's no temple to Nyx here."

"That might be part of why she's pissed," Laera said.

"It doesn't really matter, anyway. They help when they want adoration, abandon us when they're bored, and make our lives more difficult when they need entertainment." There was no point in hiding my cynicism regarding the gods. I was already on their unfavorable list.

"They're fools," Ryvin said, joining us as we watched the crew lower the plank. "And they're going to lose the whole city if they do nothing more than pray to a bunch of selfish, depraved assholes."

"You know, considering the fact that both of you are half-god, you sure talk a lot of shit about your blood," Laera pointed out.

"I'd get rid of it if I could," Ryvin said.

"I wouldn't be so quick to offer that," I said, darkly.

"Well, as nice as it is to see you two return to hating each other, I think we're going to need to play nice. We don't know what to expect here," Laera said.

"We can expect distrustful, angry humans if they aren't too absorbed in their foolish praying," Vanth said.

"Well, when the gods strike all of us down for our disrespect, I'm going to tell them I'm the only one keeping those thoughts to myself. There are some things you just don't say out loud," Laera hissed.

"I didn't realize you were so devout," I commented.

"I'm not, but in case you haven't noticed, I'm the only full fae here. I don't have any human to help me blend in and I'm not part god, either."

"I'm just a shifter," Vanth added.

"I'm not concerned about you. I'm concerned for myself," she said.

"Let's just get to the palace as quickly as possible." I walked toward the lowered plank the crew had laid for us, and without waiting to see if the others followed, I descended, making my way back to Athonian soil.

When I reached the sand, I had to swallow back the lump in my throat. I wasn't sure I'd ever return here when I'd left. Now, I was coming back with our enemy in tow to warn of an impending invasion after losing all the other tributes. It wasn't what I was hoping for. I had no good news, no hope, no reassurances for my people or my family. I was the harbinger of destruction.

I took a last look into the black abyss of the sea. Konos was invisible in the dark, the ocean leading to emptiness. In the dark, it lacked the energy and joy it used to bring. I wondered if I'd ever see the sparkling blue water again.

ATHOS LOOKED THE SAME, but different. Few buildings and homes were lit, and the streets were empty. It took on an abandoned quality and our steps seemed too loud as we made our way through town. I'd never walked this far through my own city, always having a horse or riding in a carriage. The uneven roads under my sandals were familiar and depressing at the same time. The crumbling, uneven and occasionally loose stones were a reminder of how far this once great city had fallen.

"So, this is it, the greatest human city in the world," Laera said, not masking her disgust.

"It's protected us for a long time," I said defensively.

"That's the problem, it never actually did," Ryvin said. "These walls of yours won't stop a fae army. And unless you're getting all the dragons here, I don't see things going well."

I stopped walking, and my heart fell into my stomach like a rock. "Didn't we come here to warn them? To give them a chance to defend themselves?"

"We did," he replied.

"They have us," Laera added. "Your magic and mine. Ara's would be helpful if you're willing to wield it. With monsters, we could take down ships before they even reach land."

My insides twisted. I should be the one helping with that. I should be the one learning to control that and saving my people.

"Come on," Vanth touched my arm, "I don't like how quiet it is."

We continued along the deserted street, my head turning to stare at the Black Opal as we passed. For the first time, there were no guards stationed outside its gate. It was as if the entire town was abandoned.

A heavy sense of foreboding hung in the air, the tension thick and empty at the same time. I fiddled with the hem of my tunic to give myself something to do to expel the excess nervous energy.

Something clattered and I jumped, emitting a squeak that was an odd sounding stifled scream. Vanth and Ryvin readied their weapons, and Laera raised her eyebrows at me. "Did you squeal?"

"Shh," I hushed her, then crept toward the sound, following behind the others.

A cat hissed, then raced past us, knocking a pile of crates over next to an empty shop as it ran.

Heart pounding, I blew out a relieved breath. "Just a cat."

"There really is nobody around," Vanth said, not lowering his weapon.

"They have to all be at the temples," I looked over at the Temple to Hera, the closest temple to the center of town. From there, I turned to see the Temple to Zeus, and in the distance, the Temple for Athena. It was on the outskirts of town, only visible because of the fires burning inside. Each of the three large temples had every possible light glowing. They were far enough away that I couldn't see the people who were likely gathered outside them, leaving offerings or praying, while the acolytes and priests kept the oil burning.

As we continued down the road, I kept expecting to see people returning from the temples, but they remained away. Even on feast days, offerings were left rather quickly. There were always other diversions to get to after visiting the temples. It was unsettling knowing everyone was sitting outside them, praying to the gods who didn't care about us. They wouldn't come for us. We were on our own.

Finally, I could see the palace gates. A solitary guard stood there, on the inside of the gate, rather than their usual place outside. A chill ran down my spine. After what happened at the Choosing, I wasn't sure which guards I could trust. Had those who'd turned against me been killed when Ryvin leveled the battlefield?

Glancing over at the prince, I couldn't help but feel a rush of gratitude. He'd kept me alive that day, but guilt squeezed in when I recalled the cost.

"Halt," the guard called, pulling his sword and pointing it at us.

I gestured for my companions to stay back before approaching the guard, my hands in front of me to show I was unarmed. As I got closer, I was hoping I'd recognize the guard, but he was unfamiliar. "I'm here to see my sisters," I said calmly.

The guard's brow furrowed. "Princess Ara?"

"I need to see my sister, now." I knew my clothes were ruined, my hair a tangled mess, but I held my chin high, striving for any lingering defiance.

"I'll have to ask about your guests," his words came out in an insecure stutter.

I glanced at my friends and caught Laera rolling her eyes. "Fine." She waved her hand and the guard grunted, his body tensing. He moved backward in an unnatural motion, stiff and forced.

Dark shadows slithered past me, brushing against my skin like a dangerous caress. They sent a shiver of goose-bumps along my arms and I moved aside, reminding myself that the sense of danger I felt was a warning, not something I should be enjoying. I hated that my head instantly pictured what else he could do with those shadows.

The tendrils wrapped around the gate, undulating and slithering, moving and flowing. With a thunk, the lock disengaged. The door creaked and groaned as the shadows shoved it aside, the guard struggling against the invisible forces making him maintain his distance.

As soon as we were through, I turned to Laera. "Can you release him?"

"He might try to follow us. I could just knock him out," she offered.

"They aren't your enemy anymore," I pointed out.

With an exaggerated sigh, Laera flicked her hand. The guard stumbled forward, nearly falling. Panting and panicked, he distanced himself from us. "What did you do?"

"Less than I'd have done if she wasn't here to play the hero," Laera sneered.

The guard kept his distance. "Are you going to kill me?"

"She's not going to kill you," I answered before Laera could say anything else to terrify the guard.

"Well, not right now," Laera said with a wide grin.

"Can we do what we came for, please?" Vanth said through gritted teeth.

Laera sighed, as if annoyed that he'd cut her time to torture the poor guard short.

"Come on, we have to find Lagina." I offered the guard what I hoped was a sympathetic smile, but he looked just as terrified by me as he did by my companions.

Lanterns and torches hung along the walkway and dotted the stairs that led to the palace entrance. It was the most light we'd seen in days.

We walked toward the front entryway, but we didn't get far before we reached the front to find an entire group of guards climbing down the stairs to intercept us.

"I'm here to see my sister," I said by way of greeting. "Please step aside so I can enter."

The guards removed their weapons. The largest guard stepped forward, sword extended. "That's the prince they're hunting."

"He's worth more if we capture him alive," another said.

"Still plenty for us to share if he's dead." They stepped forward as a unit, all eyes locked on Ryvin.

12

ARA

I MOVED TO THE FRONT, extending my arms to either side, blocking my friends before they could do something stupid. "Stand down, now. The prince is with me and if you touch him, you'll answer to the queen herself."

One of the guards reached me and shoved me aside so hard I landed on the ground like an abandoned child's toy.

Vanth helped me up quickly, then moved in front of me, blocking me from the guards. "She's alright," he called. I knew he was talking to Ryvin even if I couldn't see him with the giant shifter standing guard in front of me.

"That was a mistake," Ryvin growled.

I moved to the side and Vanth turned. "I'm sorry, you're not in any condition to be fighting."

"Give me a weapon." I reached for one of the knives tucked into a sheath on his thigh.

"I don't think so. Let them take this," Vanth argued, but he didn't prevent me from taking the weapon.

I didn't want any more death. I was tired of the trail of bodies we were leaving in our wake. Quickly, I feigned movement to one side, then bypassed the shifter, hurrying to where Ryvin was standing, his shadows billowing around him, a stark contrast against the flickering lantern light.

"Get out of the way, Ara," Ryvin called.

The largest guard sneered at me, his expression pure malice. "I will kill you to get to him, Princess."

"Then my death will be the only blood on your hands because you can't win against him." I glared at him, daring him to take another step. "You have two choices. You let us pass and go on to live another day, or you die a painful, slow death."

"Painful and slow?" Ryvin sounded amused. "I thought for sure you'd beg for mercy for them. I must be wearing off on you, Princess."

I ignored him, keeping my attention on the guards. Most of them were shifting their weight, their posture less sure than it had been. "Make your choice. Either way, I'll step aside, but it won't be the prince who dies here. Haven't we lost enough humans already?"

"You are a traitor. If the only death is yours, it'll be worth it," he said.

"She killed the minotaur, but sure, take your chances with her," Laera added.

A few eyes moved to me, narrowing in suspicion. I shrugged. "He killed a tribute. He deserved it."

"I think we should let them go," one of the guards said.

"Fuck that." The largest guard charged.

I dodged just as he lunged with the sword, then exploded upward, gripping my knife tightly. His eyes bulged as the blade bit into the exposed skin of his neck. Blood sprayed, and the sword clattered to the ground as he clawed at his neck. His eyes bulged and he gasped, his mouth opening and closing as he took rattling breaths.

Shadows slithered past me, surrounding me like an embrace before they reached the dying guard. They traveled from his ankles up to his torso, circling and swirling around him until he was cocooned in darkness, swallowing the gasping, gurgling sounds coming from the man's final breaths. When the shadows dissipated, the man was gone.

I was panting, my heart racing, my whole body on alert. The knife in my grip dripped crimson. "I want to see my sister."

None of the guards objected. Silently, they moved aside. Most of them bowing as we passed, a few murmuring, *your highness* or *princess* as we walked by.

Once we were inside, Ryvin grabbed my upper arm and pulled me closer to him, not slowing our pace. "How did you do that?"

"I got the knife from Vanth," I replied. "I'm not going to stay unarmed."

He grabbed me and pulled me into a hallway. Vanth and Laera stopped walking. "Give us a minute," he told them.

They took a few steps until I couldn't see them in my line of sight. I was certain they were nearby.

Ryvin moved closer, the look on his face positively feral. I stepped back, my pulse racing. When I reached the wall, he caged me in, a hand on either side of the wall near my head. I could feel his body heat and I was surrounded by his scent, the sensation making tension wind low in my belly. The things I still wanted to do with this man...

"I'm not asking about the knife," he said, a note of warning in his tone.

"I will never apologize for defending myself or my friends," I said.

"I didn't make those shadows," he said.

Now my heart was racing for a whole other reason. "What?"

"You tapped into my magic. How?" he demanded.

"I don't know." I stared at him in stunned disbelief. "I'm not sure."

For a long moment, we were silent, and I studied his face, falling into my old habit of admiring his strange and beautiful silver eyes, his firm jaw, his soft lips. Catching myself, I clenched my jaw and balled my hands into fists. He had no right to be pissed at me. "You stole my magic without asking. I'm not going to apologize for what I did."

"I'm not mad. I'm grateful. All I want is for you to live." His mouth was on mine before I could say another word.

My eyes widened in surprise for only a heartbeat before my body flared to life, making my skin tingle. Everything felt hot and cold at the same time; overwhelming and intimate; so right, and so wrong. I leaned into the kiss, my arms arcing around his neck, my fingers tangling into his hair. He pressed against me, deepening the kiss. Our tongues met and we devoured each other with desperate movements, neither of us coming up for breath.

Something dark surged within me, rising like a tide, overwhelming me to the point where I had to pull away from him, gasping for air. Shadows billowed around us, his power lingering between us like an untamed, wild thing. It pulsed and undulated, circling us like an angry beast.

Catching my breath, I swallowed hard, then brushed my fingers over my swollen lips as I took in the darkness swirling around us. As my heart slowed and my breathing eased, the shadows shrunk away until they dissipated. "What was that?"

"We're going to have to help you learn how to control that," he said.

"That was me?"

He smoothed my hair away from my eyes. "That was all you."

A thrill ran through me. I'd called on his shadows, brought them to us. Then I recalled what I'd done to that guard. The magic had consumed him. My hand stilled at my throat and dread seeped in. I looked at Ryvin. "What if I hurt someone?" It was my magic all over again. That fear of losing control.

"I'll help you." He brushed his knuckles across my cheek, and I turned away from him, moving myself from the wall.

"You didn't know this would happen, did you?"

He shook his head. "No, I didn't."

Disappointment made my shoulders slump. "This doesn't change things. You betrayed me. You took my choices from me. Just because I kissed you back doesn't mean anything."

His jaw tensed. "I understand."

"We need to go." I made myself walk away from him, knowing if I stayed behind in this hallway too much longer, I might break. I wasn't sure I'd ever be able to stop feeling things for him, but I couldn't trust my heart with someone who didn't respect me enough to include me in decisions. Especially those that directly impacted me. He stole my choice. What else might he do under the guise of keeping me safe? I wasn't a doll. I needed to be in control of my own life.

"What happened back there?" Laera asked.

"Nothing," Ryvin replied.

I tried to mask my surprise. For some reason, he didn't want his sister to know that I'd tapped into his magic. Was it possible that he still didn't trust her even though we'd agreed to work together?

We passed a few guards, but they didn't engage. I wasn't sure if it was because they knew who I was or if it was because a trail of shadows followed in our wake. The worst part was I wasn't sure if I was the one leaving the shadows or if it was Ryvin.

WE WENT STRAIGHT to my father's study, which would now be Lagina's. I had a feeling she wasn't spending her days in the throne room. Based on the six guards drawing their weapons outside the large doors, I was sure I'd made the correct choice.

We slowed and I extended my hands. "It's Ara, I'm here to see my sister." I was getting tired of repeating the phrase, but I really didn't want to see anyone else dead.

Argus stepped forward, lowering his sword. "Ara? How did you..." he lifted his weapon, "what is *he* doing here?"

"They're with me. I have to see Lagina. The Fae King is preparing his army and we don't have much time," I explained.

"I thought you might be here about the darkness," he said, his brow furrowing.

Guilt welled. That was sort of my fault. "That too."

His eyes were fixed on the others with me, his distrust obvious.

"They're here to help, Argus. Please, I need to talk to her," I pleaded.

He nodded to the guard nearest the door handle. "Let them in."

"Thank you." I didn't waste any time getting past the guards into the study. "Lagina?"

"Ara?" My sister dropped the papers in her hand. "You're alive."

"I'm alive. I just wish I had better news," I replied.

"If you were looking for good news, you're in the wrong place," she said.

"Where's Cora and Sophia?" I should have expected that they wouldn't be here, but part of me thought maybe they'd step up with everything that had happened. Or it was possible Lagina had sent them away. Insisted on doing it herself. I knew that option all too well.

"In their rooms. I don't want them involved in anything more than they have to be," she replied.

"Where's the Dragon delegation?" Ryvin asked.

Lagina turned to him, her eyes narrowing, taking him in as if noticing he was there for the first time. She returned her attention to me. "Please tell me you didn't go to Konos for a man."

I lifted a brow. "You know me better than that."

"There's nothing going on between us," Ryvin replied. "Ara has made that clear."

It felt like he'd shoved a knife into my heart.

"Then why are you here? And who are your friends?" Lagina demanded.

"You already met Vanth," Ryvin offered. "And I'm here because Ara wants me here."

"They're here to help," I said.

"And you are?" Lagina was studying Laera, not even hiding that she was taking in every detail of the princess. I had to applaud her for noticing that she was just as dangerous as the men I'd arrived with, even though Laera didn't look especially intimidating in her pale green peplos.

"You can call me Laera," the princess stepped forward, giving Lagina a sideways nod.

"The Princess of Konos?" Istvan slithered over and I didn't bother hiding my sneer. "You can't be here." He moved closer to Lagina. "She's the Fae King's eyes and ears. She can't be trusted."

"Shouldn't you be off kissing Ophelia's feet?" I turned to the priest.

The air in the room seemed to shift. As if everyone was holding their breath. My skin prickled. "What happened?"

"She's dead," Lagina said.

"Well, that's one less spoiled royal we have to deal with," Laera said.

"Laera, not the time," I snapped.

"I'm just saying what we're all thinking," she murmured.

With her powers, I had to wonder if she was speaking the truth or if she was just being, well, Laera.

"We should sit, I can explain everything," Lagina said.

"We really don't have time for a family reunion," Laera pointed out. "My father is gathering an army. He's decided he no longer needs you all around."

"We have to find out what resources we have available to defend Athos," Ryvin added.

"Why would you defend a human city?" Istvan asked.

"Because it's important to Ara," Ryvin said. "But you aren't. So watch your tone, old man."

The priest took a step back and as much as I didn't want Ryvin fighting my battles for me, I was going to let him have this one.

"Istvan, find the king. Bring him here," Lagina ordered.

"Your highness, I don't think you should be alone with them..." Istvan began but Lagina glared at him and he inclined his head, "as you wish."

"Everyone else, out," Lagina barked.

The few advisors who'd been keeping their distance hurried out after the priest. As soon as the door shut, Lagina gestured to the chairs in the sitting area. "You'll want to sit for this."

"Just tell me what happened," I encouraged as I settled into one of the chairs. Ryvin and Laera took seats on either side of me and I caught sight of Vanth moving behind me. He was the only one who didn't take a seat. I ignored the fact that they seemed to be treating me as if I needed protection from my own sister.

Lagina sat across from me, then glanced at both of the Konos royals. She fidgeted the way she did when she was nervous.

"I can explain it all to you, but I trust them. So now, what did you want to tell me?" I leaned forward.

"Sophia went into a bloodlust frenzy and killed our mother," Lagina said.

My lips parted and my eyes widened in surprise. Out of everything she could have said, that was the last thing I expected.

I wish I could say I felt pity or sorrow at Ophelia's loss, but it wasn't there. "Where is Sophia?"

"She's safe, but I don't think the rest of us are." She handed me a leather-bound book. "What do you know about this?"

My brow furrowed. "I've never seen this before."

"It was in father's room. I don't think anyone knew about it."

I wasn't sure how a journal could be more important than the impending invasion and the lack of sunlight, but I opened up the journal and looked at the first page. I recognized my father's handwriting. Flipping through, I realized he'd filled every page. Not just in nice, even lines, he'd filled every inch. Some of the writing was sideways or upside-down. There was no quickly identifiable pattern. "What is this?"

Lagina glanced at my companions. "Can we speak in front of them?"

"She'll just tell us, anyway," Laera said.

"They really are here to help," I assured my sister.

"I tried to read it all, but it's difficult to follow. Ramblings that seemed insane. When I asked Istvan, he said he thought it might be recordings of dreams or delusions. Maybe Father never recovered from his sickness after he was turned."

"But you don't think that's the case or you wouldn't be showing it to me." I peered at the pages. They were difficult to read in the dim light of the study. I'd need to sit closer to one of the glowing lamps.

"He had a whole passage about how he wanted to make stronger children." Her upper lip curled and I could see the disgust she was trying to mask. "Whole passages about bedding different women with the hopes that he'd find someone who could make his line stronger."

Nausea rolled through me, and I was certain I was wearing the same expression as my sister.

"He wrote about dead children with vampire mothers and even an affair with a dragon shifter before he met my mother," she continued. "He said the people were getting impatient, and he needed a wife and heirs."

"What if Istvan is right? What if this was all some disgusting fantasy?" I asked.

"Who is your mother, Ara?" Lagina asked quietly.

I stilled. Until recently, I would have been able to honestly tell her that I didn't know. Having a goddess for a mother wasn't going to gain me favor in a human city, and I no longer had any of the gifts that came from her. "You know he never told me."

"I think you know," she said.

"Does it matter?" I asked.

"Only because I need to know if this journal is accurate," she replied.

"Why?" Ryvin cut in. "What did you find in there?"

"Don't stop her, brother. I'm enjoying the gossip," Laera said.

I shot a look at the princess, but she simply smiled at me.

"Unless it's more important than the army of fae heading our way, I think it could wait until we find out if any of us survive the next few days," Vanth suggested.

"That's the problem," Lagina said with a sigh. "It can't wait. It says he got a warning about one of his elder children. A half-human daughter who would fight in darkness and either save the world or doom us all."

"Rantings of an old man," Ryvin said.

"I thought the same, but then the sun vanished," Lagina said.

"It could be anything," I commented. "That's so vague."

"It had the mark of the Oracle next to it. I think he saw her and got the prophecy from her." Lagina turned to me. "Just tell me you're human and I'll know it's not true. It can't be Sophia, she's the youngest and it can't be me because I'm human. Ara, who was your mother?"

13

MY STOMACH TWISTED. How many times was I going to hear the same thing? I couldn't be that important in the scheme of things. It didn't seem possible. All I did was fail.

Unless I was destined to bring it all down.

"Ara? Just tell me," Lagina repeated.

I glanced at my friends; they all wore blank expressions. No warnings, no sympathy, no encouragement. They were letting me make the choice.

"I don't know if I want to answer that," I admitted.

Lagina's shoulders sank. "How long have you known?"

"I found out after I left Athos," I said.

"Do I want the details?" she asked.

"Probably not," Laera cut in. "If you can't handle your other sister being a boring half-vampire, you certainly can't handle Ara's heritage."

I shot Laera a glare. "That's not helpful." The princess

shrugged, and I returned my attention to my sister. "It doesn't matter, anyway. Anything that came from my mother is gone. That part of me was removed. I'm just human."

Lagina's brow furrowed. "I don't understand."

"It's complicated." I wasn't about to go into all the details. "I don't think that prophecy means much of anything. Half of what comes out of the Oracle's mouth is nonsense."

Lagina still looked tense, but she took the book from me and set it down. "Then how do you explain the fact that the sun is gone and the fae are on their way?"

"Well, Nyx is responsible for the sun," I began.

She waved her hand. "I know about the prison. Somehow, the Dragon King knew. Not that my advisors gave me that information until it was no longer helpful. What we don't know is how she got out or what her plans are."

"She wants revenge on the humans," Laera said.

"Could you maybe not?" I hissed.

The princess sighed. "This is taking far too long. Look, Ara killed the Minotaur and released Nyx. The goddess was furious that humans forgot about her and vowed revenge, but she's sleeping now. The Fae King is not. He's the greater threat."

Lagina's jaw dropped and she stared at me as if she'd never seen me before. "You what?"

"I told you it was complicated." I offered a small smile.

"Complicated is whatever you're doing with the Konos Prince. Freeing a goddess and killing monsters is hero-level stuff. The kind of thing that gets you added to prophecies."

"It doesn't matter. Maybe I set it all up to end," I said, voicing my fear, "but I can't do anything anymore. I'm useless. Anything that made me special is gone."

"That's not true," Ryvin said.

"Don't," I snapped.

The door opened and a large man walked in, strolling into the room as if he owned the place. Lagina stood. "I assume your entourage alerted you to our visitors since I don't see Istvan." She looked over at her guards. "And my guards couldn't manage to get you to knock before entering."

"Your guards know I won't harm you," he replied.

"It's called manners," she shot back. "Knocking. Maybe that's not a thing in Drakous?"

I stood. "So, this is the famous Dragon King."

"And you must be the brave sister. The one who went to Konos." He took in the others in the room. "I see you brought back some souvenirs."

"Did I hear correctly? You're the one who released Nyx?" He settled into an open chair without waiting for an invitation.

"You could hear that in the hallway?" I asked.

"Dragons have excellent hearing," he replied.

"They just can't shift in Athos," I commented.

He lifted a brow.

"You can't shift here?" Lagina asked.

The king was still staring at me. "You seem to know a lot for a sheltered princess."

"You'll find that the Princesses of Athos are full of surprises," Ryvin said.

"I am discovering that," the king said.

"This isn't getting us anywhere," Lagina said. "If you can't shift and the Fae King is on his way here, what are we supposed to do? We don't have enough soldiers. The city walls are only going to hold for so long."

"Wait till you hear how the king can't even be killed," Laera said, her tone amused.

Everyone turned to her.

"What? I'm just saying what we're all thinking. Unless we can take out my father, we're not going to be able to win. We don't have the numbers, but they won't fight under his banner if he's gone," she explained.

"Nobody is invincible. Even the Fae King," the Dragon King said.

"I watched him survive more than he should," Vanth said. "He's supposed to be protected by magic."

The Dragon King stood. "I'll be taking my bride and heading back to Drakous." He turned to Lagina. "As her next of kin, you are welcome to reside with us."

"What?" I was standing now, not remembering making myself move. The shock of his words was too strong. "You can't possibly mean..."

"He's betrothed to Cora," Lagina said as if it was an afterthought.

"You couldn't have led with that?" I accused.

"Little busy with trying to keep us all alive," Lagina snapped.

"You sure you want to bring these ladies into your home?" Laera asked.

"If you're done arguing, I have a solution," Ryvin said.

Everyone looked at the prince. "The magic that was used to restrain Nyx would have been very powerful. It's likely the cause of the limited magic in this city. If we can free it, we should gain the ability to wield it better here."

"I suppose you won't tell us why you released her in the first place?" The king grumbled.

"It was because my father stole her magic to make himself more powerful," Ryvin said simply. "We were trying to defeat him."

"You failed," the king pointed out.

"Clearly," Laera said, not masking her annoyance. "You sure are living up to that rumored dragon intelligence."

"I don't like you," he said with a growl.

"Get in line," she snapped.

"Enough!" Vanth cut in, silencing the whole group. We all looked at the shifter.

"It sounds to me like we have two options. We either abandon this city and flee, or we try to unlock some of that magic and fight. Would you agree?"

We were silent for a moment, then all of us nodded.

"Good. Then what's it going to be? Leaving Athos or trying to save it?" Vanth looked at each of us, staring us down.

"We can't get everyone out," I finally said. "They'd never make it all the way to Drakous. And that's assuming they'd take a bunch of human refugees."

The king growled. "I'd let in anyone who survived the journey."

"I can't imagine the numbers would be great," Lagina said.

"Humans are fragile creatures," Laera added.

"Maybe if your kind wasn't slaughtering us for entertainment..." Lagina began.

"You'd slaughter each other if we didn't. Don't act like you're all blameless and kind to one another," Laera cut in.

Lagina pressed her lips into a tight line, and I knew that she was seconds away from losing her temper completely.

"It's been a long day. Or whatever this is." I glanced

toward the window, noting that it was still just as dark as it had been before, then returned my gaze to my sister. "We should get a short rest, then see if we can find the magic. If it's not possible to release it, or whatever we have to do with it, we can start evacuating Athos."

"Why are we waiting for rest?" The Dragon King asked.

"Because humans are fragile," Laera repeated.

I shot her a dirty look. "I need some rest. I don't speak for all humans."

"I don't even know if it's morning or evening. Or the last time I slept. I never really thought about how much we rely on the sun," Lagina said wistfully.

"Are you tired?" I asked, noticing how she looked so much older than she had just a few short days ago.

"I'm not sure," Lagina answered. "I don't think I get the luxury of being tired."

"I understand." I moved closer to my sister so I could wrap my arm around her and I pulled her in for a sideways hug.

"We'll go to the caves while you sleep," Ryvin said suddenly.

Vanth stood. "I really hope Selena fled town."

"I hope not. She's our best chance at finding information," Ryvin said.

Laera stood. "Catch me up on whatever you know on the way there."

"I'm joining you," the Dragon King added.

Ryvin, Laera, and Vanth all turned to look at the king. "I think we've got this," Laera replied.

"You could use all the help you can get if you want any chance of saving this city," he pointed out.

"Tell us why you care again?" Laera asked coolly. "An alliance with Athos does nothing for you. You're weakened here and adding a human to your line doesn't help you."

"My reasons are my own," he said, his tone a low, growling sound.

"Oh, stop it. This is ridiculous. If we're going to work together, you have to stop having a pissing contest. He says Cora is his mate. Whatever that means, it's important to him," Lagina said.

My stomach twisted into guilty knots. I knew how it felt to have a powerful being tell you that you're meant to be. That feeling that came from the expectation of losing your choice. The deep knowing inside that made you question everything because even if you didn't want to be drawn to him, you were.

"Alright. He can come. But his mate stays here with you," Ryvin said.

"Good. I want her as far from the magic we hunt as possible," the king responded.

"You should go, then," I encouraged. The last thing I needed was them to see me fall asleep on my feet and I had one more thing to tend to before I slept.

Ryvin hesitated and I could tell he was considering saying something, but he ended up just nodding, then left the room. Laera and the Dragon King followed.

"Be on alert," Vanth said. "I think there's more going on than we're aware of."

"I will." As soon as they were out the door, I turned to my sister. "Where is Sophia?"

14

Ara

ARGUS FOLLOWED us silently as we walked down the hall. It made me feel a little better knowing he was going to stay with Lagina through all this.

As soon as we were away from the guards still stationed at the study, I turned to Lagina. "What can I expect here? Is she still herself?" It was my greatest fear. Her gentle heart and innocence were a refreshing reprieve from the constant power struggles of the palace.

"She's struggling to adjust," Lagina offered. "We all are."

The guards outside Sophia's door were all familiar. It was nice to know that some of the older guards had survived, though I couldn't help but wonder if they were actually loyal.

Lagina knocked. "Soph? It's me, Gina. I have a surprise for you."

We waited a few heartbeats before the door opened a

crack and, after looking both ways, Lagina squeezed inside. I followed and Argus closed the door behind us.

The room was so dark, it took my eyes a moment to adjust before I could see the outline of both figures. "Sophia?"

She gasped, then a candle flickered to life, and I saw the smile on her face seconds before she collided with me. My sister held me tight, her arms squeezing me around my neck. Her whole body shook as she sobbed into my hair. "You're alive. You're alive."

I smoothed her hair, caressing her head the way I used to when she was small. "It's alright, I'm here. I'm safe."

Suddenly, she broke free of my embrace, distancing herself quickly from me. "But you're not safe. Not in here with me." Her eyes darted around wildly, her expression pure panic. "You have to get out of here. You can't be here. I could hurt you."

"You're not going to hurt me," I assured her.

"You haven't hurt anyone else," Lagina said. "It was an accident. It won't happen again. You have what you need now."

"No." Sophia shook her head. "Ara, you have to convince them to send me to the Underworld. I can't be here. I can't be around regular people. I'm a threat. A danger. A monster."

"You're not any of those things, or you'd have harmed me the moment I walked in here. Instead, you gave me a hug," I reminded her.

She tensed, her brow furrowing as if considering my words.

"None of this is your fault," I added. "We didn't know, so we couldn't prepare. How could you be to blame? You were a child. It wasn't your choice."

"It was me who took my own mother's life," Sofia's voice cracked as she spoke.

"They have ways of preventing that from happening," Lagina said. "If we'd known..."

"If we'd known, they'd have killed her," I said.

My sisters both looked at me, each of them with wide eyes. "Don't act like it's a surprise. We all know how everyone in this kingdom views anyone who isn't human. We were raised to fear all others. The fae, the vampires, the shifters. Even the gods. You think a half-vampire child would be allowed to live?"

Sophia's hand moved to her chest and she looked down, taking slow breaths. I'd never seen her look so conflicted.

"I'm not excusing him for what he did," I added. "But we can no longer afford to ignore the fact that we were raised to view the world a certain way. To maintain the illusion of safety this city provided. To play the part."

"That's why Aunt Katerina was sent to the wall," Lagina said softly.

"What?" My aunt had always been my inspiration. "She didn't volunteer?"

Lagina shook her head. "Her other option was a temple."

I balled my hands into fists, ignoring the bite of my finger-nails in my palms. I should have known. I should have seen the parallels. I was so blind.

"Everything was a lie, wasn't it?" Sophia said softly.

"Yes," I replied without hesitation. "And that's not your fault. So you aren't going to pay for their mistakes."

"My mother..." she took shaky breaths, "she's gone. That's my fault."

"No more blame. You're going to figure this out. I don't

want to hear excuses, you understand?" I had never spoken to her so harshly, and her surprised expression nearly made me take it all back. But I knew it was the only way she was going to listen. Ophelia never sugar-coated anything when it came to orders.

"You will get the craving under control and we will figure out what this means for your life moving forward. We're not losing anyone else, you hear me?" I stared her down, unblinking.

Finally, she nodded. "Alright."

I tried to hide my relief, but I felt my shoulders drop as tension left. "Now, what can we do to help her?" I asked Lagina.

"Istvan has some texts on the way and the Dragon King seems to know some about how to help her," she replied.

My jaw ticked at the mention of Istvan. If it were me on the throne, he wouldn't be breathing. I still didn't trust him, and I never would. "It sounds like help is on the way."

"They're making me drink animal blood," Sophia added quietly. "It seems to help."

"See? We'll figure this out." I moved closer to her and took her hand in mine. She gave me a small smile and I could almost see the girl she'd been when I left hiding behind those hollow eyes. I knew I'd never see her return to who she was before. Like me, there was no going back. But she'd grow to be someone else. Someone more powerful.

I'd always looked at her as so fragile, but there was a stronger woman under that innocent facade. None of us let her challenge herself to find that strength. We couldn't coddle her anymore.

"We're going to need your help," I said. "It's possible you'll be stronger and more powerful with that new part of you awakened."

"Ara," Lagina hissed. "She's not getting involved in anything."

"I want to help," Sophia challenged.

I smiled. "I know you do." I was surprised I had never seen it before. There was another side to her that we'd all neglected to see. We didn't let her step outside the box we'd placed her in. "Once we figure out how to help you control the hunger, we can focus on finding out how you can use this to your advantage."

"You'll let me help with the darkness?" she asked.

"Who better to help with darkness than a vampire?" I replied.

For the first time, I saw a genuine smile and I knew she was going to pull through this. It wasn't going to be easy, and she would never be the same as she had been, but she was going to emerge victorious.

"How's Cora taking it?" I asked as Lagina and I walked down the hall toward my room. It was odd traveling down the familiar route but not seeing the typical familiar guards.

"About as well as you'd expect," Lagina replied. "I think she honestly thought she'd get to marry Tomas."

"How'd he take it?" We were moving slowly, taking our time. "Did he come crying to you? He seems the type to beg."

"No, I never heard any objections from him." She sighed. "I was a little disappointed for Cora. I know she'd have wanted him to fight for her. At least some."

"Has she tried to run yet?" I asked.

Lagina laughed. "Where would she go? She would never join a temple, and she can't exactly flee to Drakous."

"He's really her mate?" The concept would have been impossible to me even a week ago, but now it only seemed impossible that he found her.

"That's what he says." Lagina stopped in front of my door. "Nobody touched your room. It's exactly as you left it."

"I wasn't gone all that long," I pointed out.

"My mother wanted to empty it the day you left," Lagina said.

That sounded exactly like Ophelia. It was hard to believe I'd never see her judgmental stare or listen to her nasty comments again. I tensed, realizing that also meant the child she'd carried was also gone. Lagina had lost a mother and a sibling. "I know I wasn't always kind to your mother, but I really am sorry for her loss. I'm sorry for you and Cora and Sophia. None of you should have to go through that."

Lagina took my hand in hers. "I know. And I know you knew more than anyone what it's like to have that empty place where your mother used to be."

Guilt made my insides tighten. I never experienced it as deeply as she would since I had never met my mother, but then it turned out my mother was never actually dead. I wasn't even sure if she could die. For a moment, I considered telling Lagina everything. There'd been a time I wouldn't have hesitated.

"You should get some rest. I'll send someone to wake you when the others return." She gave my hand a squeeze, then released it. "It's nice to have you back home, Ara."

"Thanks, Gina." I gave her a smile, but it was forced. The

word *home* rolled around my mind, not feeling like the correct term for what this place now was.

Entering my room was like being somewhere you'd outgrown long ago. Like trying to fit into clothes you'd worn as a child. Someone had lit candles, illuminating the space with a soft, flickering glow. Everything looked the same. It even smelled the same. It really hadn't been that long, but it felt like stepping into another world. How had so much changed in such a short time?

I considered washing off the grime of travel, but made the mistake of sitting down on the edge of my bed. Now that I was alone and still, I could feel everything. Every ache, every bruise. All the exhaustion. All the sorrow and heartache.

Letting myself feel it all, I curled up on my side and hugged my knees to my chest. I don't know if I cried or if I fell asleep before the first tears fell.

15

RYVIN

THERE WERE a few lamps lit in windows as we walked through the abandoned streets. Some of the people must have tired of offering their tidings to the gods. Or they were running out of offerings to give. There wasn't as much smoke in the air as there had been. I wondered if the gods were laughing while they burned the few resources they had while their crops died from lack of sun.

"How did you get Nyx out?" The Dragon King asked as we walked. "I know you didn't come through town."

"I don't see how that's any of your business," Laera replied.

"It is if you want my help," he said.

"I'm not sure we even asked for that," Laera shot back.

"We used a portal," I said. "And no, we don't need your help, but if you were the one leading this, I'd want to know."

"So, you can be reasonable," he said. "After everything I've heard about you, I wasn't sure."

"It's not like your reputation is pristine," I pointed out.

"No, but I know the rumors about me are mostly true. So if that's the case for you, I am aware of what I'm getting into. Especially since we all know my magic is limited in Athos." He stopped walking, and I paused, wondering what he was getting at.

Laera let out a long sigh. "Please don't have a dick-measuring contest right here. I can't handle that."

The Dragon King gave her a sideways glance, then looked back at me. "I know your power outweighs mine. And I also know that the only reason either of us cares at all about this city is because it houses the family of the women we're... attached to."

"Attached to?" Laera rolled her eyes. "What a hopeless romantic."

"There's no guarantee of love between mates. We all know that. Especially you two, after what your father did to his mate," the Dragon King said.

"Who said anything about mates?" I asked.

"It's obvious. She might not want you, but I know you have no choice in keeping her safe at the very least. There's no other reason you'd be here helping these humans," the king replied.

"Is there a point to all this?" Vanth asked, moving closer to me. The shifter was about the same size as the Dragon King, and it was likely the king knew that the wolf's shifting abilities weren't hampered in Athos.

"The point is that for now, we're on the same side. Which means we have to watch each other's backs. At least temporarily. Otherwise, none of us will trust the other and we're never going to have a chance at protecting this city."

"I'm not your friend," I said.

"I'm not asking you to be," he replied. "But if we can't ally for this, there's no point. We might as well start the evacuations now."

"You're boring me," Laera said. "Are we going to find the magic or not?"

"I'm serious. Outside of Athos, I could take you all down without effort. Even you can't withstand dragon fire. I know I'm vulnerable here and I'm not risking my life or my mate's life for this city," he said. "I will take my mate and leave this city to its demise."

"Fine, we won't kill you, is that what you want to hear?" Laera said.

The king growled.

"We're on the same side. For now." I took a step closer to him, then lowered my voice just in case anyone was peering out their windows. We'd been here too long and if anyone happened to look, we'd be drawing attention. "But you can't be stupid enough to think what happens in Athos won't impact you. He doesn't care about Athos. He wants Drakous. Always has."

"He can't hold my city," the king replied.

"That won't stop him from trying." I crossed my arms over my chest. "I might be wrong here, but I'm pretty sure your people also need the sun for survival."

"What does that have to do with the fae? I didn't anger Nyx," he said.

"No, she's got nothing against the dragons. At least not right now. But the longer she keeps the sun hidden, the longer we all go without crops. In Konos, they can grow without sunlight. We've adapted to the lack of sun. I don't think Drakous has," I pointed out.

"Are you threatening my people?" He took a step closer to me and I could almost smell the brimstone I always associated with dragons.

"I'm not threatening. I'm telling you we have greater problems. And we can't help you with Nyx if we're all dead," I said.

"Maybe the goddess would be appeased if Athos was gone. It is the city that housed her prison," he said with a shrug.

"Perhaps. But I've never seen her as the forgiving type. If she can't take that anger out on the humans in Athos, she'll find them in other places. Other kingdoms where they live freely. Places like Drakous."

"Now you really are threatening my kingdom," he said.

"Oh, for fuck's sake," Laera said. "Do you know who he is?"

The king glanced at Laera. "The Prince of Konos? Is that supposed to mean something?"

"He's Nyx's son, you dumb dragon. If anyone has a chance at calming the goddess, it's him." She shook her head, clearly annoyed. "Now, if we're all done with the threats and the throwing our weight around, can we please move on with our work? I'd rather not meet my end in this lousy human city because you brutes couldn't get your shit together. Now, agree not to kill one another while our goals align, and we can move on with our lives."

"Honestly, she's probably the most dangerous one here," Vanth said. "You might want to listen to her."

"I'm not afraid of a spy," the Dragon King said, though he did step back from me.

"Keep underestimating me," Laera said with a smile. "It makes it easier for me when nobody takes me seriously."

"You know what those women who live in that palace value above all else? Including your mate?" Vanth suddenly cut in, ignoring Laera.

"Each other," I answered, even though I knew he wasn't talking to me.

He glanced at me, then looked back at the Dragon King. "That's exactly it. You want her in your bed? Make sure her sisters don't die."

He grunted, then nodded. "Fine."

I started walking again, anger and annoyance making my whole body tense. I wasn't expecting all this when I came to Athos. I figured I'd find out if my mother was truly here and start working on a plan to free her. I didn't count on feeling obligated to protect the city from my father's wrath. In all honesty, I thought he'd be dead.

In the darkness, the Black Opal didn't look as grand as it had when I'd visited with Ara. Laera made a light, sending the orb in front of us as we neared the arched entryway. The guards were absent, and we walked into the courtyard. In the glow of Laera's light, the plants already looked wilted, and the fountains weren't running. It looked like it had been abandoned for much longer than the sun had been gone.

"You said this is Selena's place?" Vanth asked.

I nodded.

"Where is she?" he asked. "She doesn't seem the type to be on her knees for the gods."

"She might if she doesn't want anyone to know what she is," Laera said.

"Selena? Not the famed assassin?" The Dragon King asked.

"She's supposed to be dead, but apparently we can't even trust the afterlife anymore," Vanth said.

I paused at the entry, noting that the beaded curtain was gone. In its place was a rather sturdy looking wood door. For a moment, I considered knocking. Instead, I reached for the handle. When it turned, I looked over at Laera and Vanth, my brows lifted in silent surprise.

Laera shrugged, then inclined her head. Vanth drew his weapons. I opened the door.

The interior was lit with a few scattered orbs of light. Without the crowds and the smoke, it looked dingy and ancient. The tile floors were cracked, the few rugs were threadbare and gray, which probably wasn't their original color. The cushions that had been full of people were covered in stains that made me wrinkle my nose.

"Selena wouldn't be caught dead in a place like this," Laera said.

"I have to agree with the princess," Vanth added.

"It looks better when it's full of people who bring gold," a smooth, clear feminine voice cut in, as the proprietress entered the large room. Her long silver hair was in a knot on the top of her head, making her look taller than she already was. With her brown skin and large dark eyes, she could be Laera's sister. Nobody would guess she was much older. I could see how she'd succeeded in gaining entry to anywhere she wanted. With beauty like hers, most men wouldn't stop to question her presence.

"I thought I killed you," Vanth said.

"I thought I told you not to bring that dog into my establishment," she said, her brows raised.

"I need both of you right now," I replied.

"You left us," Laera said, not masking the accusation in her tone.

"I didn't have a choice." Selena glanced at Vanth, then turned her attention on my sister. Growing up, the assassin had been like an aunt to Laera. She'd tolerated me, but she'd doted on my sister.

"You left me with *him*." The energy in the room shifted, and I struggled against a sudden surge of anger. Laera was letting her magic get the better of her.

"Pull it back," I bit out.

The feeling dissipated quickly, but the damage had been done.

"That was interesting," the Dragon King said. "I see your magic isn't muted here."

"I don't know what you're talking about," Laera said.

The king scoffed. "I felt that, Princess. I knew you were a spy; I knew you got the information you needed, but I didn't realize you could make everyone feel your emotions."

I almost let my relief show, but held it together. He was so close to discovering what she was capable of, but he didn't realize she was so much more powerful than that. We'd never discussed her magic, but I'd picked up enough over the years that I had a good handle on what she was capable of. And it was terrifying.

The king stepped closer to Selena and the assassin held her ground, her chin high. He inclined his head in greeting and I blinked a few times, surprised by the exchange.

"Mistress Selena, I'm pleased to meet you. Though you've killed many of my friends over the years, I can respect your talent." He lifted his head. "I'd be honored to have you in a temporary alliance with us."

She lifted her brow, then looked at each of us in turn. "You're all working together?"

"So, it seems," I said reluctantly.

"I assume you're here about Nyx," Selena said.

"Not quite," Laera answered.

"The king is heading this way with every ally he can summon," Vanth explained.

She tensed. "I left that island for a reason."

"And what reason was that exactly?" Laera bit out the words as if she'd been holding them in for hours.

"Your mother knows," Selena said.

"You used me to fake your death," Vanth blurted out.

She shrugged. "I needed an escape that would be believable."

"Mother? Is everything alright?" A young woman came around the corner and my eyes widened. I had thought Laera and Selena could pass as sisters, but this woman was practically my sister's twin.

Violet eyes, long silver hair, stunning brown skin. Even the way she moved was like a copy of the steps my sister took.

"Who the fuck are you?" Laera asked.

The woman looked at Selena, then took in all of us. I could see her hands shaking. She looked like a rabbit that had been cornered. While she might have the physical appearance of my sister, she didn't have any of her fearlessness.

Selena sighed. "Well, now you know why I left."

"Is this, is she..." Laera struggled to get the words out. I'd never seen her speechless.

"Did he hurt you?" Vanth asked.

"I'm not discussing this with you," Selena replied.

"What's your name?" The king addressed the woman, his courtly manner showing in his kind smile and gentle demeanor.

The woman seemed to relax a little as she turned her attention to him. "I'm Vera."

"Lovely to meet you, Vera." The king inclined his head politely.

"She's your sister," Selena confirmed, her eyes locked on Laera. Then she looked at Vanth. "And no, it wasn't my choice."

"I should have killed *him* that day," Vanth said with a growl.

"You'll get your chance," I said.

"No, he won't," Laera said. "Because I'm going to kill him first."

16

Ara

SOMETHING CRASHED and I woke with a start. The whole room shook, drawers rattled, the candles flickered, my bed vibrated... I scrambled off the bed, sure I was dreaming, or imagining things. A candle crashed to the floor; the flame snuffed out by the marble floor.

I hurried over to the other candle and grabbed it from the desk, working to maintain my balance so the light wouldn't go. Dust fell from the ceiling and the rumbling continued while I contemplated if I should leave my room.

Before I could decide, the shaking stopped. My heart was racing, and I was panting as if I'd been running. I'd never experienced anything like that before, but I'd read stories about the earth shaking. Had the gods come for us? Were the fae here already?

Carrying the candle with me, I reached the door just as it swung open. An unfamiliar guard stood on the threshold. I tensed, prepared to defend myself if needed, but he was practically doubled over while he caught his breath.

"Are you alright?" I asked.

He sucked in another breath, then blew it out before straightening his posture. "Your sister sent me to check on you. I ran."

"I'm fine. What was that?" I asked.

He shook his head. "I'm not sure."

"Where is she?" Whatever that was, it couldn't be good.

"Study," he said through gasping breaths. He was an older man, and I wondered if he'd done a less active job before joining the guards.

"I'll walk you there," he offered.

I nodded, then stepped out of my room, closing the door behind me. I wasn't sure how long I'd been in there. The lack of sunlight was making it much harder to determine time. All I knew was that I felt more rested than I had, but I wasn't sure if that was due to the excitement or if I'd actually slept for a while.

"What's your name?" I asked the guard as we walked.

"Everyone calls me Hal," he replied.

"Thank you for coming to check on me, Hal," I said.

"I was honored. You know, not all of us think what you did was so wrong," he said casually.

Now I knew he hadn't spent much time here. The guards who would speak so friendly with us were rare, and that usually came after getting to know each other. Like David. Or Belan. My chest tightened and I swallowed down the grief. How many more was I going to have to mourn before this was over?

"I heard he came back here with you," Hal continued. "The prince. Is that true?"

"Yes. He's helping us against his father." I knew better than to give that kind of information to a guard I hardly knew. That was the kind of thing my father would have insisted should be discussed behind closed doors.

"Good thing you two took a liking to each other while he was here. Can you imagine what would have happened if he wasn't changing sides for a woman? No offense, Princess, I just can't imagine how much worse this would be if he was charging in with his father," Hal said.

I didn't want to explain how much more complicated everything was. Or how I wasn't sure if Ryvin's magic was going to be enough to help us when the fae and their allies stormed our shores. But he had a point. If Ryvin was working with his father, we'd have no hope.

As I approached the study, I was joined by a few advisors who were also on their way to visit my sister. They didn't seem to share Hal's enthusiasm at my presence.

"Open the door, Argus," I said, ignoring the gathered advisors who were waiting around the door for permission to enter.

The guard obliged, and I didn't mask my dislike of the men standing in the hall as I entered.

Lagina was pacing the room. Istvan stood in the corner watching her. They both looked up at me. My sister ran to greet me. "You're safe."

"I'm safe. Sophia and Cora?" I asked.

"They're good. I checked on them on my way here," she explained. Their rooms were in the opposite wing from mine. Another way Ophelia had separated us.

"What was that?" I asked.

"The gods are angry," Istvan said darkly.

"Are you sure? Is that why there's no sun?" I didn't mask my sarcasm.

"What do you want us to do? We've given the offerings; we've consulted all the books..." Istvan actually sounded afraid.

I stared at the priest, unsure if I'd ever seen him show any kind of emotional response other than contempt. "Wait, all you've tried is giving offerings to the major gods. The ones we have temples for, right?"

"We left smaller offerings for others." He was right back at contempt.

I resisted rolling my eyes. "What about Nyx? Anything for her?"

He opened and closed his mouth a few times. I covered my face with my hands, annoyed at myself for not thinking about this sooner. Lowering my hands, I faced the priest. "Nyx is angry because she thinks humans forgot about her. And we're proving her right by not doing anything for her."

"There's never been a temple to Nyx," he said.

"That's the point. She's not honored. And despite the fact that she's the goddess of night, nobody thought to contact her or appease her when we went into eternal night." I couldn't believe this wasn't the first thing I asked about when we arrived.

"We need to build her a temple," Lagina said suddenly. "A grand temple."

"And how exactly are we to do that?" Istvan asked.

"Figure it out," she demanded. "Find the masons and the architects, get the supplies. If nothing else, we should be well on our way to starting it if the goddess shows up to destroy us. If she sees we're trying to correct the wrong, perhaps she'll have mercy."

If Nyx was like the other gods, that was a good plan. There was a real chance that she'd be thrilled with the prospect of being honored with a new temple.

"What are you still doing here?" Lagina said. "Go."

Istvan bowed, then bolted for the door, leaving it open when he left. I could see the advisors still crowding around the entry, waiting for admission into the study.

Lagina smoothed her hair back, then took a deep breath. "Gentleman, please come in."

I made my way to the window and peered outside, distancing myself from the conversation Lagina was having with her advisors. They were certain that the shaking was a warning, and they all had different ideas of what she should do in response. None of them were good.

As I watched the darkness, I stopped listening to the discussion. The sky was dotted with stars, constellations whose names I learned when I was a child but had forgotten. I wondered if I should learn them again now while they were on permanent display.

"Excuse me, your highness," Argus's voice broke me from my stargazing.

Everyone in the room was facing the doors. The guard bowed, following protocol, which I knew was for the sake of the advisors. "The Dragon King, and the Prince and Princess of Konos have returned."

"Let them in," Lagina said.

The advisors gasped, their voices suddenly rising as they talked over each other with a variety of complaints.

The Dragon King, Ryvin, Vanth, Laera, Selena, and a woman I didn't recognize walked into the room. They were coated in thick white dust.

"What happened?" I asked.

"And who are these new people?" Lagina asked, crossing her arms over her chest defensively.

"You remember Selena," I gestured toward the proprietess of the Black Opal.

"It's been a while and I hear you have a new title," Selena bowed low, "your highness."

Lagina tensed. "I didn't recognize you, I'm sorry."

Selena rose, then brushed some of the white powdery dust from her arms. It didn't do much to change the coating of the thick powder. She was covered in the stuff, making her look almost like a ghost. "Allow me to introduce my daughter, Vera."

The woman bowed, following her mother's lead. "Your highness, it's an honor to meet you."

"She's another sibling," Laera said, not sounding happy about the revelation.

"There's three of you now?" Lagina didn't mask her unease. "So she's, I mean, you're not human?"

"Fae, same as us," Laera confirmed.

"Welcome, Vera." I tried to sound warm, but my tone was stiff. The awkwardness in the room was contagious.

"Are you here because you're fae, or because the Black Opal is involved?" Lagina asked.

"The prison was under the Opal," I explained.

"Why am I not surprised," Lagina said with a sigh.

"Does that mean you found the magic? Did you unblock it?" I asked eagerly.

"Oh, we found it alright, but it's not going to be released easily," Ryvin said.

"Your father was a crafty one," Laera said as she settled into a chair, a cloud of dust rising around her as she sat. "He knew what he was doing."

"It's trapped very well. There had to have been a sorcerer involved in holding all that in place." Ryvin shook his head.

"It explains why magic is so limited for most of us," the Dragon King said.

"Well, can you fix it?" Lagina asked.

"Please tell me there's a way we can release it," I added.

"There's a way, but none of us can access it," Ryvin said.

"What does that mean? Do we have to give in? Run?" That was the last thing I wanted to do. Even if we fled, what would prevent the Fae King from chasing us until he eliminated us all?

"We need a vampire," the Dragon King blurted. "Most likely, one with a blood relation to your father."

"You want Sophia to help?" Lagina sounded horrified. "She's in no condition to go anywhere."

"She's our only option," Ryvin said. "There's more magic holding that in place than I've ever seen in one location. It was essentially set up with a blood lock as the first step. Once we're through that, we can access the rest and we should be able to release the magic."

"She'll do it," I said. "I know she'll want to help."

"If that doesn't work?" Lagina asked. "What happens to her if you're wrong? What happens if she can't get through?"

"You don't want to know," Ryvin replied.

"I will not consent to something that might get my sister killed," Lagina said.

"It's too bad you didn't have the same concern about Ara," Laera said haughtily.

Lagina rounded on the princess, and I could almost feel the anger rolling from her in waves. I grabbed her shoulder and pulled her back. "Stop it."

"I did not ask you to go," Lagina said.

"But you were going to send Sophia," I reminded her. "She would have died."

"I made a mistake," Lagina said. "I will not risk any of you again."

"That's not your decision. Sophia can decide for herself." I took my hand off my sister's shoulder. "You can't control everything."

"Why can't it be done without her?" she asked, turning to Ryvin.

"Your father was already a vampire when he sealed in the magic. It's not going to work with human blood." He glanced at me. "Or Ara's."

Lagina pressed her fingertips to her temples and closed her eyes. When she opened them, she looked at each of us. "Before my father died, the closest I got to magic was the heated water in my bath."

"You might be surprised what kind of magic you'll see when we release it," the Dragon King said.

"I'm not sure I'm ready for that," Lagina admitted.

"You need to prepare," he warned her.

"The books," I said, recalling the locked tomes. "The ones behind the portrait."

Her brow furrowed. She didn't know. Quickly, I explained about the hidden books that I'd once tried to read. "If there's anything about what it used to be like here, it might help you prepare."

"I don't think that's a good idea, your highness," one of the advisors cut in.

I turned to him, startled by his interjection. I'd forgotten they were there. All of them were standing near my father's desk. Lagina's desk, now, I supposed. They'd been listening, letting us plan and discuss.

"And why is that?" Lagina asked.

"Because they know," Laera said. "And most of them are on someone else's payroll."

17

ARA

"GUARDS!" Lagina shouted.

The doors burst open, and Argus and the other guards stationed outside crashed into the room.

One of the advisors drew a weapon and launched toward Lagina, but Ryvin was faster, moving in front of my sister with flawless grace. He dodged the man's attack, then stabbed him in the side before disarming him.

The advisor fell to the ground, clutching at the gushing wound. He hissed curses as he glared at Ryvin. The prince held the blade to the man's throat. "Try anything and I'll finish what I started."

The other advisors stepped back, eyes wide with shock.

"She's lying," one of them shouted. "We're loyal to Athos."

"Arrest them all," Lagina ordered.

"Your highness," one of them protested.

"You trust that Konos witch over us," another hissed.

"We've served your father for years," someone else said. "We're loyal to Athos."

Lagina hesitated, as if trying to reconcile the fact that she was taking the word of Laera over her father's advisors.

"Should I tell her which of you let the maid in who tried to kill Ara?" Laera asked.

Ryvin moved in front of me, shadows rising around us. "Who was it?"

"What is she talking about, Ara?" Lagina asked, without taking her eyes from the men.

"I was poisoned by the servant who replaced Mila," I confessed.

She glanced at me. "You never told me."

"She nearly died," Ryvin added. "Which of you is to blame?"

Carlin, a younger advisor who'd been serving my father for only a few years, ran.

Ryvin moved with his shadows, cutting off the man's exit before he could reach the door. Before any of us could react, the prince had his knife in the man's throat.

Blood poured from the wound and the man collapsed to the ground, a crimson puddle spreading on the floor.

"Take them all to the dungeon. I don't want to hear any excuses." She pointed at the other advisors and showed no signs of compassion. She was pure malice, and I didn't blame her. These weren't people she'd chosen. They were more remnants of our father's rule.

The men protested as Argus and his guards took hold of them, handling them with the same roughness they would any criminal. "Don't give me a reason to send you to the Underworld," Argus threatened.

"What about that one?" Argus asked at the doorway, lifting his chin toward the man on the ground.

"We'll handle it," Laera offered.

The men quieted as they were hauled away, their whimpers and sniffles muffled by the footsteps of the guards.

Ryvin's shadows returned, surrounding the fallen man. When they dissipated, the body was gone. I shivered, recalling how I'd summoned that power, even if I didn't know how it worked or where exactly the dead were sent.

Then he walked toward the man he'd stabbed in the side. The man was struggling for breath, whimpering and begging for mercy. "Want me to finish him?"

My sister turned to Laera. "I've heard about you. Your skills are legend around here. What do you know about this treacherous snake?"

Laera stood, then casually walked toward my sister. "You might not be as weak as I thought you were."

"Underestimating me would be a mistake," Lagina said.

Laera smiled and kept her gaze locked on my sister. "He's been reporting to my father for years. But he's not alone. One of them reports to me, another to the vampires in Thebes, and one reports to him." She tilted her head toward the Dragon King.

"Are any of them loyal?" Lagina asked without flinching.

"Only one, but that's only because they haven't yet reached his price. Not because he chooses to stay loyal." Laera yawned, covering her mouth, then turned away as if this were the most boring conversation she'd ever had. "Is there anyone who can bring us something to eat? I'm famished."

"What should we do with him?" I asked, staring at the man bleeding out on the floor.

"He's dead either way. You can let him suffer, or end it quickly," Laera said with a dismissive wave of her hand.

Lagina stared at the man while he sucked in rattling breaths. Ryvin's hand was steady, the blade positioned just above his throat.

"Gina..." I couldn't believe she was contemplating this. "End it."

She hesitated for several more heartbeats, and just as I considered giving the order myself, she nodded at Ryvin. The prince moved the blade quickly and the man made a sickening gurgling sound, his body convulsing once before he stilled.

I wasn't sure I recognized my sister anymore. But then again, I doubt she recognized me. Everything had changed in such a short time.

"Everyone should dress for dinner," Lagina announced. "We'll reconvene in the formal dining room."

"No words for me?" the Dragon King asked.

Lagina moved closer to him, stopping just before they'd touch. "I was working on how to place my own informants in your court. And then you showed up and asked to marry my sister. At this point, I'd say our fates are intertwined, whether we like it or not."

She turned, then walked away from him, stopping at the door. "Formal dress, I think. This could be our last family dinner for a while." She pushed the door open, then left.

The Dragon King chuckled. "If Cora is anything like Lagina, I'm always going to be on my toes."

"Lagina's predictable," I said. "Cora is wild, untamed. You will never break her or pin her down."

"Good," he said. "Now, I suppose I should find a bath. I'm guessing our appearance is why the queen gave us time to dress before dinner."

"When she said everyone, did she mean everyone?" Vera asked timidly.

"Yes, I believe she did," I said. "I'll show you to a guest room where you can clean up."

Ryvin was wiping the bloody knife on his dusty tunic, leaving a red streak that would normally be hidden by the dark fabric. When our eyes met, a shiver ran down my spine. I looked away before I could overthink my feelings for him.

SELENA AND VERA insisted on having a room that wasn't near Laera's. It took a while, but I finally found rooms that were well stocked enough for all their needs.

"This room seems adequate, though I suppose there won't be any black tunics for you to change into," I told Ryvin as I gestured to the room next to his sister's.

"If you think I'm going to let you go to your room alone, you're insane," he said.

I crossed my arms over my chest. "I was in my room alone while you were crawling through clay dust, or whatever that is all over you."

He looked down at his tunic, then back up at me. "That was before I knew just how infiltrated your father's court was by enemies."

"It was your people," I reminded him.

"My father's people," he countered.

"Isn't Laera in charge of all that?" I asked.

"She's usually the one in control, but the fact that none of your father's advisors was truly loyal to him is astonishing. He must have made enemies wherever he went," Ryvin said.

I was trying to think of more arguments for why Ryvin couldn't come to my room, but I was already walking. "You know they could've come for me while you were gone. Why would they come for me now?"

"Because we outed them," he said.

"This feels like a stretch. Are you sure you're not just trying to get into my room?" I asked.

He shrugged.

"That's what I thought." I was still furious with him, but I was beginning to thaw. Not that I wanted to. I wasn't sure it was going to be possible to stay angry at him forever. Maybe it was a good thing that all of us were likely running on borrowed time.

We stopped in front of my room. "You do realize I'm not getting in the bath with you."

"It's not big enough for both of us." He opened the door and gestured for me to enter.

I lifted a brow. "Well, thank you for inviting me into my own room."

He smirked, then followed me in. When he closed the door, the light from the lamps burning in the hallways was extinguished, leaving us in absolute darkness.

Panic spiked and my pulse raced. I turned, reaching for the door handle when light appeared.

Lots of light.

Dozens of small, floating lights sparkled and winked

around the room. They were just like the lights I'd seen in the woods on Ceto's island. Beautiful and playful, the lights flickered and floated, casting a warm glow around my room. The whole space became magical and inviting.

As dangerous and deadly as the fae were, there was so much beauty in what they could create.

"I won't bother you while you bathe," Ryvin said. "But I am going to wait in your room to make sure you're safe."

I walked toward the bathing chambers, stopping before crossing the threshold. I turned to Ryvin. "For what it's worth, I'm glad you're not dead."

18

ARA

THE LARGE WINDOWS overlooking the sea were a reminder of how much had changed. The endless expanse of blue was gone. Replaced by fathomless black. Empty darkness untouched by the faint light of the moon. Stars twinkled, their cheerful sparkle almost mocking at this point. If not for them, I wouldn't know where the sea ended and the sky began. I was growing very tired of endless night.

Servants bustled around the room, finishing table settings and filling wine glasses. It was the first time I'd seen any servants since returning to the palace. I wondered how many had fled after the Choosing. It was likely they knew exactly what happened here. What my father was, why Mila and the others had died.

What Sophia was.

The grief swirling was twofold, a deep sense of loss for all those who'd traveled to the Underworld and grief for my sister. She'd lost so much and then she'd lost her humanity.

"Ara, you'll sit on my right," Lagina announced as she swept into the room. "We will offer the other end of the table to the Dragon King since he's the highest-ranking visiting royal." She glanced at Ryvin. "Unless you'd like to claim it despite the fact that you are planning regicide. Perhaps we're dining with the future King of Konos?"

"I don't need the head of the table," he said, ignoring her obvious attempt to find out his plans for the succession of Konos.

Before the conversation could get any more awkward, the Dragon King entered. He paused in the arched entryway and scanned the room. Selena and Vera approached, and the king moved to let them pass.

"Welcome," Lagina said. "Please, everyone have a seat. We have much to discuss over dinner."

The room went silent and a cold chill passed through me. Turning, I saw Sophia hesitating at the entry. Argus and another guard stood on either side of her.

She looked smaller and frailer than I'd ever seen her. Her skin pale, her long blonde hair almost white, her blue eyes too large for her thin face. The pale blue peplos wasn't helping, the soft color adding to the faded quality of her form.

"Thank you for coming, Sophia," Lagina said gently.

She nodded, then moved forward gracefully, taking her usual place along the back wall in the center of the long table. The guards took the seats next to her, surrounding her.

It was an unusual group. Selena and her daughter sat opposite Sophia, while the Dragon King and Lagina took the heads of the table. I sat next to Lagina and Ryvin took the place beside me. Vanth sat next to him, leaving an empty chair between him and the guard next to Sophia.

"Where's Cora?" I asked.

"She's late," Lagina replied.

"Should I fetch her?" The Dragon King asked.

"Why would you do that?" Lagina asked cooly. "She's probably avoiding this dinner as a way to protest the arrangement. You trying to force her into a meal is only going to cause her to rebel more."

"She's going to be a queen," the Dragon King mumbled. "She better learn how to do things she doesn't want to do."

"She will do her duty when the time comes," Lagina assured him. "Give her this little bit of control before she loses her home."

"Not everyone is thrilled to find out they have a mate. Especially when they grew up not even knowing mating bonds were a thing," I explained.

"Are you talking about your sister or yourself?" the king asked. "Mating bonds are sacred. They should be honored."

"Bonds don't matter. You can't own another person. If your mate doesn't want you, figure out how to move on." Ryvin picked up the glass in front of him and took a long drink.

I hated the warmth that spread in my veins from his words. If only I could actually trust them.

"We're not here to discuss Cora," Lagina said as the servants began to add platters of food to the table. They added plates of roasted fish, bowls of fresh vegetables, baskets of sweet honey cakes, and platters of fresh figs.

It was a stark contrast to the darkness outside. All this

fresh food from the gardens and orchards seemed too luxurious when I knew the plants they came from were dying.

"Please, take what you like. Then we'll talk," Lagina offered.

She dismissed the servants, having them leave casks of wine on the table before departing. We served ourselves, as if we were at a family meal, the intimacy either a necessity for secrecy or a ploy to get our gathered group to drop their guard. Either way, it was a smart move on my sister's part.

I added a couple of figs and some of the vegetables to my plate but declined the other offerings. The thought of eating while we were in the midst of such serious business made my stomach turn. I glanced up at Sophia and noted that her plate remained empty. She didn't quite look like herself. Her skin had a grayish ashen hue, her sparkling blue eyes were flat and downcast.

"You should try to eat something," I encouraged, sliding the plate of honey cakes her way.

She looked up at me. "Can I even eat anymore?"

"I've seen other vampires eat," I said.

Everyone at the table seemed to suck in a collective breath.

"She's not going to hurt anyone." I didn't bother to take my eyes off my sister. Shoving the plate of cakes closer, I nodded to her. "You're fine. Eat something."

She reached for a cake, her hand shaking slightly as she did. The cake looked so small on her large plate, but I didn't want to push her to add more food. For now, if I could get her to eat that, it would be a start.

Lagina cleared her throat, and we all turned to face her. My sister, the queen of Athos. It still didn't feel real.

She lifted her glass. "Before we begin, a toast to those we've lost, and to those we will lose along the way."

Everyone joined, lifting their glasses. We drank. The only sound was the glasses being set back down on the table. The room was so still and heavy with unanswered questions. We waited. I took another drink.

"As you all know, the Fae King is on his way here," Lagina began. "Our new allies, the Dragons," she inclined her head toward the king, "cannot shift into their other form in Athos to help us fight the fae unless we find a way to fix it."

Sophia's eyes widened and she let out a gasp. She didn't seem to notice that the rest of us weren't reacting. "What can we do? We can't fight the fae on our own. Even with our soldiers returning from the wall."

"There's a way we might be able to gain the ability to shift," the Dragon King said. "But we'll need your help."

"Mine? You can't want me to help. I'm too much of a risk," she said.

"You're exactly what we need," I cut in.

"The only way we can release the magic is to break the magic your father used to seal it in. And we can't do that without someone of his bloodline," the Dragon King explained.

"Why me?" Sophia asked softly, glancing at Lagina, then me. "Why can't my other sisters do this?"

"That's the additional security your father added," the Dragon King said. "We need someone with vampire blood."

"You're the only one who can do this," I added.

"That's why you're having a dinner?" Sophia asked.

"We can't do this without you," Lagina replied.

Sophia picked up her glass and sipped the wine, then she

wrinkled her nose before setting the glass back down. "It doesn't sound like I have a choice."

"I'm sorry," Lagina apologized, sounding like she meant it. That was a rare thing from her, and it was probably the only reason why Sophia's tense expression softened.

My youngest sister let out a heavy sigh. "Fine. But I can't make any promises."

"We just ask that you try," Lagina said.

"And if you fail, your entire city will be destroyed," Laera added with a shrug.

My eyes widened. "Laera," I snapped.

"She deserves the truth. Even if everyone else around here is coddling her." Laera turned her attention to Sophia. "Listen, Princess, you're more powerful now than you were. You're stronger, harder to kill, faster, you'll see better in the dark, and honestly, within a few days, you'll be basically irresistible to any human you come across. You'll have strengths you never dreamed of. And they have to let you embrace them so you can grow."

Sophia's face looked a little green. "I didn't ask for any of that."

"None of us asked for the gifts we have." Laera glanced at me, likely recalling the time she'd told me the same thing.

"I know it's overwhelming," I told Sophia.

"You don't know anything," she hissed. "You left us. You left me. It was supposed to be me. If I'd changed on Konos, I'd have killed them, and my mother would still be alive." She stood so quickly, her chair tumbled to the floor. "The only thing you ever consider is how you can be the hero. It doesn't matter the impact it has on anyone else, as long as you get to step in to save the day."

"Soph…" I stood, but she tore from the room, moving so quickly that she was already through the door before I stepped away from the table.

"That went well," Laera said.

I threw her a dirty look. "You riled her up."

"I told her the truth," Laera shot back.

"She needed to hear that," the Dragon King said.

My brow furrowed. "What? Why would she need to hear all that?"

"Because she'll start noticing changes and if she doesn't have any warning, it could be very overwhelming. Especially for someone who seems so sensitive," he said.

"She's going to be fine," Lagina declared. As if her word was enough to alter the very stars.

"I should go talk to her," I said.

"No, you shouldn't," Ryvin set his hand on my arm. "Give her some time. She'll agree to help and that's what we need right now. You can make up with her if we're all still alive when this is done."

"I'll talk to her," Cora's voice came from behind and I turned to see her standing in the doorway.

"How long have you been there?" Lagina asked.

"Long enough," she replied, then turned her gaze to me. "I'm sorry I didn't greet you sooner, Ara."

I walked over to my sister, and she threw her arms around me. "I'm glad you're alive."

"It's good to see you too," I told her.

She released me from her embrace. "You need her to do something with magic?"

I nodded.

"Alright. I don't understand it, but I'll talk to her," she said.

"Thanks," I replied, knowing she was the only one who had a chance to reach Sophia right now.

Cora glanced at the table and I caught her looking at the Dragon King for just a heartbeat before she turned and left.

When I looked back at him, his body was so tense I thought he might explode from his chair. But he remained, his eyes still locked in the place where Cora had been.

I returned to my place at the table, even though I had no desire to eat.

"Sophia will come around," Ryvin whispered.

"I'm sure she will. She'll want to help," I agreed.

"I'm not talking about that. She was just angry. She doesn't blame you for what happened to her mother," he said.

I swallowed hard, then nodded. I knew it wasn't my fault. I knew she wasn't a vampire because of me, and I knew I'd left to save her. But if there was a way I could have spared her the pain she was going through, I would.

The worst part was the only reason I was sad Ophelia was gone was because of the impact it had on her. I'd sacrifice her a hundred times if it meant keeping my sisters safe. It was the only thing I'd ever been charged with, and I'd taken my job seriously. To the point that I had put that above all else. I was exactly the person she thought I was.

And I was starting to wonder if it was worth it.

19

ARA

"ARE you going to give me the details about what happened earlier today?" I whispered to Ryvin.

The dinner guests were eating quietly, the only sound the scraping of silverware and dull thud of glasses being returned to the table. It was the most awkward meal I'd ever eaten.

"Not here," he replied, matching my whisper.

"I didn't realize the Black Opal was so connected to all my father's misdeeds," Lagina said.

"Oh, Selena and misdeeds go way back," Laera said.

"You can say that again," Vanth mumbled.

"I can assure you, the location of the prison was coincidental." Selena took a dainty bite, seemingly unbothered by the conversation.

"I'm not even sure of all the details here, but I'm going to say that's a lie," Lagina cut in.

Selena raised a brow. "Am I being accused of something, your highness?"

"Of course you're not," Ryvin said.

"I can answer for myself," Lagina said without even looking at the prince. "I'm learning that nothing around here is as it appears. I don't care what your story is, I just know that there are no such things as coincidences, and I know there's no way you're human. Honestly, you're far too beautiful. I should have known years ago, but I was foolish and believed what I was told."

"You don't owe her an answer," I said.

Lagina gave me a sidelong glance, then returned her attention to Selena.

"It's fine. I know what it's like to be lied to. Betrayed by those you held closest to your heart," Selena began. "I came here a long time ago, before you were born. Before your father was king. But I took over the Opal at his request. As a favor."

"Payment or due?" Lagina asked.

"Due," she replied. "Unfortunately, he passed before I called it in."

"Then I will owe you one, but I will insist on using my discretion as to granting it," Lagina said.

"That is very kind, your highness." Selena inclined her head.

"He asked you to protect the prison?" Lagina guessed.

"Only after an attempt to free the goddess was made," Selena confessed.

"How did he know about you?" I asked.

"I never asked," she admitted.

"You're fae," Lagina said.

Selena nodded.

"Well, isn't this lovely? I think you might be the only human at the table," Laera said.

Lagina trained her gaze on me then, a silent pleading in her expression.

I hadn't yet confirmed with her who my mother was or what she was, but it seemed like we were letting all the secrets out now. I didn't want to keep this from Lagina any longer. "My mother is Ceto."

"Fuck." Lagina huffed out a breath, losing her poise. At that moment, I saw my sister. Not the queen, not the ruler of the city, but the sister I used to explore the city with. The sister I snuck into the Black Opal with. The sister who used to know all my secrets. How had we lost all that in such a short time?

"She has no magic, if that's why you're concerned. It was taken from her, so she's basically human now," Laera said.

"You're just trying to create drama at this point, aren't you?" Vanth growled.

"Maybe. This has to be the most boring dinner I've ever attended," the princess admitted with a shrug.

"Laera," Ryvin bit out her name like a warning.

"We're back," Cora announced.

The bickering stopped, and we all turned to see my two youngest sisters waiting in the doorway.

"She's going to do it, but she's got conditions," Cora announced.

"Tell us," Lagina said, her tone gentle.

Sophia stepped forward. "I want *her* to teach me how to use this to my advantage." She pointed to Laera.

I had to force myself to close my mouth. That was not what I expected.

"I know why you left, Ara, I do. But I deserve the chance to do something for this family and if I can be strong enough to help, I want to help," she said.

"That's impossible," Lagina said. "You're not a fighter. You never have been."

"Yes, she is," I said, wondering why I never saw it before. There was something there, under the timid sweetness. We just never noticed it. Or never gave it a chance. We'd shielded her because she was the youngest and the sweetest of us.

"Are you forgetting that I'd need to agree to that as well?" Laera asked. "I never volunteered to teach a half-vampire how to be a vampire. I have absolutely no experience with that. And I am not nice."

"You were the only one willing to speak to me like I could be something more," Sophia said.

"I'm not sure you want her training you," Vanth added.

"What's that supposed to mean?" Laera practically snarled.

"She's a good teacher," I said. "She'd be good for Sophia." And perhaps some of Sohpia's sweetness would wear off on Laera. But I wasn't about to say that part out loud.

"You sure you want your sister around Laera?" Ryvin asked quietly.

I shrugged. In the end, it wasn't my choice. Sophia was asking and Laera was the one who would decide.

We watched the princess, waiting for her to respond. She had her arms crossed over her chest and was glaring at Sophia as if she'd offended her by asking such a thing.

Sophia didn't know anything about magic, and I was

guessing she'd not heard Laera's reputation. Though based on the determined expression she wore, I wasn't sure she'd care if she did.

With a long sigh, Laera dropped her arms to her side. "Fine. But only if you actually survive all this. Of which there is no guarantee."

"Good. Then you have yourself a vamp—" Sophia closed her eyes, then swallowed hard. She took a deep breath, then opened her eyes. "You have yourself a vampire."

"Does that mean this dinner is complete?" Selena asked.

Lagina stood. "I want you to return to free the magic as soon as possible."

"Let's get this over with," Laera said, rising from her chair. "I'm bored and could use something more entertaining than hanging around this palace."

Ryvin stood, followed by Vanth. I joined them, ready to get this done.

"You need to stay here," Ryvin said.

I laughed. "You know me better than that."

I'D GIVEN up trying to determine what day it was or if it was morning or evening. We'd eaten dinner before exiting the palace, but it could be breakfast time for all I knew. I wasn't sure if anyone had successfully kept track and it had only been a short time. At least I think it had been a short time. It was unnerving not knowing. I wondered if that was part of the punishment from Nyx. Humans were meant to have sunlight and darkness. We couldn't survive with too much of either.

We weren't alone this time as we moved through the streets. Curious onlookers peered through windows, candles flickering inside their dark homes. Some of them hid from sight at our approach, others called more people over to watch our progress. I could hear their whispers but couldn't make out the words.

In the cover of night, I wasn't sure we could be identified, but a group our size traveling by foot together would draw enough attention on its own. Twice we were approached by another small group, but both times they'd turned around before speaking. I wondered if Laera had anything to do with that or if they'd simply decided we weren't worth the trouble.

There were parts of Athos that weren't safe to travel alone at night. That had always been the case. But now, I wasn't sure there was anywhere that would be safe for people to go. Once we figured out this magic thing and defeated the king, I had to find a way to return the sun. Though, I was certain that facing down Nyx was going to be far worse than anything the Fae King could throw our way.

The Opal looked disappointing in the dim moonlight. As if it were a memory of itself. The once proud exterior took on a foreboding quality. Had it always looked so daunting? The white structure was gray in the darkness and the roof melted into the sky, a patch of starless black.

"Please don't do anything stupid," Ryvin whispered as we crossed under the archway leading to the garden in the courtyard.

"And what exactly would I do that would be considered stupid?" I inquired.

"Coming here is a start," he said. "But I can't very well ask you to travel back to the palace alone with so many people out on the streets."

"You do know I'd be better protected if I still had my magic," I reminded him.

"You win. Alright? Whatever you want, you win," he said, his tone exasperated. "Just please be careful. The fact that you don't have your magic is exactly why I'm concerned."

He pulled me aside, next to the statue of Dionysus. The water in the raised cup wasn't bubbling or flowing anymore, it just sat there, stagnant and depressing, like everything else in the garden in the darkness. Dion would have hated it.

The others filed past us, making their way through the doorway into the Opal.

"What are you doing?" I hissed.

He leaned down so close I thought he was going to kiss me, then he spoke quietly, "If anything goes wrong, you run. You don't worry about me or anyone else. You run."

"You know I won't do that," I reminded him. "Especially not with Sophia here."

"I'll make you a deal," he said. "If I tell you to run, you run for yourself, and I'll take care of Sophia. I will do everything in my power to protect her and get her out of here. But I can't help both of you. If you won't run, I will leave her behind so I can carry you out of here myself."

"You wouldn't dare," I hissed.

"You know I would." His lips were nearly touching mine now and heat burned low in my belly. I could smell him, and I recalled the taste of his kiss, the feel of his hands on my skin. I wanted to run my fingers through his hair, feel his hard chest pressed against me, hear him groaning in pleasure.

"You drive me insane," I said, because I couldn't say what I wanted to say. I couldn't tell him all the ways he made me feel.

He licked his lower lip slowly and my eyes followed the movement, recalling just how good that tongue felt against my skin, just how soft his lips felt against mine. I nearly melted into a puddle right there and had to brace myself against the statue.

My body responded, tension and anticipation winding tight like a spring. It took everything I had to resist grabbing his tunic and pulling him against me. "I hate you sometimes, you know that?"

He grinned. "I know. Now, let's get down there before they try to figure it out without us."

I stepped aside and gestured for him to go in front of me. He led us to the stairs I'd taken the day I brought him here. I recalled the way he'd looked with the water running down his naked body, then cursed internally for allowing myself to continually conjure images of him that I shouldn't. He was a distraction I couldn't afford, and it was as if it was getting worse with each passing moment. When we were finished with this, I probably needed some time away from him. But I wasn't sure we'd get that luxury. It was possible the Fae King was already on his way here.

20

ARA

THE CAVES WERE as I remembered them with one exception. The torches that typically burned in their mounts on the wall were dark, replaced by glowing orbs of light magically floating around the space. At some point, I might get used to the magic that accompanied the fae I was spending all my time with.

Ryvin's hand brushed against mine as we followed the group and my heart fluttered in response to his touch. I didn't reach for him, but I didn't pull away, either.

We quickly caught up to the group, who were making their way past the pools toward a hallway I'd never been down. Laera and Sophia were in front, with Vanth and Selena behind. The Dragon King had stayed with Lagina at the palace in case they needed protection once we unleashed the magic and Vera was upstairs, with specific instructions to keep everyone out of the Opal.

"So this is what's down here," Sophia said, a note of awe in her tone. "It's beautiful."

"This is your first trip to the Opal, isn't it?" I confirmed.

She hummed in agreement. "I wasn't allowed. It seems funny now, how well protected I was considering how dangerous I am."

"You're not dangerous," I countered. "You'll gain control of this, and you'll be fine."

"I don't think I want to be fine," Sophia countered. "I think I want to be dangerous."

"I like this girl," Laera said, amusement in her tone.

"Can we focus on getting the job done?" Vanth asked.

We continued through a hallway I'd seen servants emerge from. I figured it led to a storage area, but as we got deeper into the tunnel, I found we were inside another labyrinth of caves and tunnels.

"How large is this space?" I asked.

"I haven't explored it all," Selena admitted.

I could feel a hum of something, a pull. Instinctively I traced my fingers along the wall on my right. "It's through there, isn't it?" I asked quietly, lifting my chin toward the tunnel ahead on the right.

"You can feel it?" Ryvin asked.

"Yes."

"This way," Selena announced, turning down the tunnel toward the pull I felt.

"What is that?" Sophia asked. "It's like a tingling. Or slithering. Or something."

"You're feeling the magic. It's trying to break free, so it'll only get more intense as we get closer," Selena explained.

"How come I've never felt this before?" Sophia asked.

"I couldn't feel it until recently, either," I added. "You get more used to it, but it's still strange."

Vanth stepped in front of my sister. "Stay behind me. I'm not sure what we're going to find as we get closer."

"We found a wall, shifter. You were there," Laera said.

"And we pummeled the wall before giving up and leaving. If anything was left to guard it, we didn't make it happy," Vanth replied.

"He's got a point," Selena said.

"I thought you hated him," Laera said.

"Doesn't mean I can't agree with him on this. We're talking ancient, powerful magic all held back against its will. Magic wants to be free. It doesn't like to be trapped or sent where it doesn't belong," Selena said.

A chill ran down my spine. "Just how much magic is trapped down here?"

"Enough to prevent a half-god from finding out she wasn't human," Laera said. "I suspect it's why your mother really stashed you here. Without wild magic, yours never manifested."

"So, what happens when we release it?" Sophia asked.

"Nothing good, I'm sure," Vanth replied darkly.

"We don't have a choice," Ryvin added.

Turn after turn, we traveled through the tunnels. I didn't have to question how they knew the way. With each step, the magic seemed to sing in my veins. Growing stronger as we approached. I knew the others could feel it calling to us, urging us forward. As the magic intensified, the sense of foreboding increased. There was a warning in the sensations, a hint of caution. Something telling me to turn around even though I knew we were on the right path.

Though the tunnels were narrow, Ryvin never left my side. I hated how comforting his presence was. With my anxiety rising as the magic did, I wasn't about to send him away. It was nice to have him next to me, knowing his shadows were on my side since my magic was gone. I might have weapons with me, but I knew how little damage they could do against most magical creatures. And this wasn't a creature. This was pure magic. How could I defend myself against that?

Knots twisted in my stomach and nausea built, the sensations of the rising power making me feel off balance.

"It's fighting back against us already," Laera said. "Maybe it doesn't want to be free."

"It doesn't know we're here to free it," Selena said. "Magic is a wild thing."

"I'm not sure I can continue much longer," Sophia said.

"We're almost there," Selena encouraged.

Sure enough, our next turn took us to a dead end. The cave swirled in my vision and I felt like I was on a ship, rocking in the waves. White dust covered every surface, making my sandals slip as I walked with uneven steps. Chunks of white marble littered the ground, the remnants of whatever they'd done the last time they'd been here.

"This is it," Laera announced. "We got through the first layer, but we found this."

I moved closer, keeping my hand on the wall for balance. Ryvin grabbed my elbow. "Let me help you."

He seemed steady on his feet, unaffected by the energy I was feeling. "Why are you fine?"

"The more magic you have, the less you feel it," he replied.

My jaw tensed and I glanced at the rest of our party. I seemed to be the only one so badly affected. Everyone else was walking normally. I wondered if anyone else was desperately avoiding throwing up.

"You can go back," Ryvin said quietly. "Nobody will think less of you."

I shot him a dirty look and he pressed his lips together, likely keeping his thoughts to himself.

A bronze circle with our family crest was mounted on the white marble wall in front of us. It practically glowed with a strange gold aura.

"Is this it?" Sophia asked, brushing her fingers over the bronze medallion.

Laera pulled out a dagger. "Yes, and now, for the fun part."

"What is she doing?" I could barely get the words out. Breathing was getting difficult, as if something heavy was pressing into my chest.

"Blood magic," Ryvin said.

Selena backed away from the wall and Vanth followed, leaving just Laera and Sophia by the medallion. Ryvin wrapped his arms around me, and I was feeling so weak, I didn't fight him. My vision was blurring and I was feeling so tired. I knew I needed to get out of here, but I couldn't make myself move to leave.

"You ready?" Laera asked.

"Just do it," Sophia said.

Laera took Sophia's hand and cut a long slice down her palm. My sister winced but didn't cry out. I think I told her I was proud of her, but I wasn't sure if I said it out loud because she didn't look my way.

She was so focused on the task, she didn't seem to be

aware of anything around her. Slowly, she reached out toward the medallion, the blood from her palm leaving dots of bright crimson on the ground.

I swayed and Ryvin held me tighter. He smoothed my hair back. "You want me to take you out of here?"

I didn't respond, I was too focused on Sophia. She pressed her palm to the medallion and a trail of blood dripped down the white wall. When she pulled her hand away, there was a gruesome mark on the bronze, but it didn't stay for long. The blood began to move, filling in the grooves around our family crest, the ruby liquid moving along the recessed spaces like a red river. Then the medallion turned, rotating in a slow circle. When it stopped, there was a rumble, then the wall began to slide to the right, revealing a passage beyond. Dust fell around us, the ground shaking as the door vanished into the recessed space.

When it stopped, we were left with an empty black abyss. Magic came rushing out, making my heart race. I gasped for breath as the crushing weight of it made my vision blur. Gripping Ryvin's arm, I struggled to keep myself upright, but as the door continued to slide open, my breathing grew more ragged. The whole world was tilting, and I struggled to keep my eyes open. From somewhere far away, I thought I heard Ryvin calling for me, but I couldn't see him. I couldn't feel him. Then everything went black.

21

Ara clawed at my arms, her breaths coming out in struggling gasps. I held her tighter, fear squeezing around my chest, making it difficult to breathe. "Ara, stay with me."

Her eyes darted around wildly and she gasped for breath. The panic in her expression shattered me. I shouldn't have let her come. I should have made her stay behind. Not that she'd have listened to me. Ara collapsed in my arms. Her entire body went limp.

Something roared from the darkness, and I looked up to see gold eyes staring back at us. The fae lights flickered, their glow weakening as the creature from the depths beyond stalked toward us. I was not going to let her die here. Not from the crushing magic spilling out to us, and not from the beast heading toward us.

"Ara, please, hang on. I'll get you out of here." I turned, not caring that something was growling from the darkness. Not caring that I was leaving everyone else behind.

Suddenly, all the fae lights were extinguished and we were thrust into a void.

"Ryvin!" Vanth called.

I heard the distinct sound of him unsheathing his sword.

Growling and the sound of claws against stone echoed through the darkness. I could feel Ara's heartbeat, her warm breath. It was steady and strong. She was fighting against this.

Sophia screamed and someone ran past me, their hand brushing against me as they made their way back. I suspected it was Selena, not waiting to stick around to face the beast we'd unleashed.

"Princess, get to the wall, follow it away from my voice," Laera called.

"We need light," Vanth ordered. He didn't have the magic to create the orbs.

"No lights," Laera replied. "It's not working. We're fighting blind. Try not to stab me, shifter."

"Ryvin, where are you? Can you cut through the dark?" Laera demanded.

I hesitated, knowing Ara was in serious danger in this state. I considered taking her and running. I could imagine her waking, watching the light return to her eyes; then the anger she'd lash out once she realized I'd saved her and doomed everyone else. I'd lose her forever if I saved her now.

"Fuck. Yeah. I'm on my way." Her morality was wearing off on me.

I set her against the wall, hoping she'd wake on her own and that I hadn't just left her as a snack for whatever creature we were facing.

Stretching my hands out in front of me, I called my shadows. "Weapons close, don't chase it. You might stab someone."

"Where's Ara?" Vanth asked.

"Down," I replied.

He grunted and the beast roared. I knew he'd struck it, and I hoped it wasn't swallowing him whole as I wasted time summoning my shadows.

I could feel my magic rising and I knew it was swirling around me, moving through the darkness as if it belonged here, as if it was part of the chaos we were occupying.

Wild magic flowed around us, and I called to it, summoning it to me, using it to strengthen my own darkness. I could feel the others in the room. My shadows closing around them, guiding me toward our foe.

When they found their target, I sent all I had toward the creature. It hollered, crying out in an ear splitting howl as I tightened my grip on it. "Back up. I've got it!"

I heard shuffling and I knew my sister and my friend were free of my magic. Using everything I had, I drew my hands together, making the shadows crush the creature, calming it, and sending it back to the Underworld.

The lights flickered back to life, but the heavy weight of magic remained. I raced to where Ara was still unconscious on the ground and felt for a pulse. My shoulders sagged in relief when I found that she was still alive. She was unharmed and her heartbeat and breathing were strong.

"What was that?" Vanth asked. He had a large gash down the side of his face, blood dripped down his neck and onto his tunic. The sword in his hand was coated in a crimson so dark it was almost black.

"I'm not sure," I admitted.

Laera held daggers in each hand, her body tense as she stared into the darkness of the passageway ahead. "Whatever it was, I'm guessing it wasn't alone."

Sophia was shaking, her face almost as white as the wall she was pressed against. "I think I changed my mind. I don't know if I can fight things like that."

"Sure you can. You just have to remember that you're one of them now," Laera said.

Sophia went even more pale. "I'm nothing like that creature."

"You're a predator, darling. It's a good thing. You don't have to blindly attack like that monster did. You get to choose when you unleash yourself," Laera said. "You're still you. The things that matter to you are still there."

Sophia was still shaking, but she looked a little less tense. "But I killed my own mother."

"You won't let the monster within ever win again," Laera said gently.

My brow furrowed slightly. It was odd seeing a softness like this from my sister.

I turned my attention back to Ara, brushing the hair that had fallen in front of her eyes away from her face. She looked so peaceful. Like she was simply sleeping.

"Selena took off, I see," Vanth said.

The fae assassin was nowhere in sight, but that might be for the best. She led us down here, but it didn't mean we could trust her. "Don't worry about her. Let's just finish this and get back to the palace."

"You don't think that was it?" Laera asked. "I've never felt this much magic."

"It's still here, though. It's not leaving the tunnel." The whole passage was thick with magic. As if it was still trapped, leashed somewhere in the depths of the darkness ahead. "I don't think this is all of it."

"Of course it wouldn't be that easy," Vanth said.

"I'll stay with Ara and Sophia," Laera volunteered.

"No, I'll take them back, you two go on," I replied.

"Are you kidding me? You've got your shadows and her ability to control monsters and water. You're far more useful with whatever is down there," she said.

"If anyone's less useful, it's me," Vanth said begrudgingly. "I was swinging at air." He shook his head.

"Fine. Take the princesses. We'll finish this," Laera said.

"What if you need me again?" Sophia stepped away from the wall. Most of the color had returned to her face.

Laera glanced at me, a silent question in her expression. I nodded once. My sister turned to the new vampire. "If you're up for it, we'll take the help."

"I can do this. I just got flustered," she explained.

"We aren't born with the ability to face down things that terrify us," Vanth said.

"Thanks," Sophia replied. "Take care of Ara, will you?"

Vanth had already lifted Ara from the floor and was holding her like a sleeping child in his arms. My whole body reacted as jealousy screamed through me. I wanted to remove his head from his body for the way he was touching her.

"I recognize that look, old friend," Vanth said. "I'm keeping her safe, not stealing her from you."

My nostrils flared and my jaw was clenched tight. Hands balled into fists, I had to fight against the need to destroy the shifter holding Ara.

"Get over it, brother," Laera hissed. "If Ara wanted the bulky shifter, she'd have had him already."

"I'm not sure that's helpful, Princess," Vanth murmured.

"We have things to do, and you can either let him get her to safety or you can ask him to carry her behind us into harm's way," Laera reasoned.

I blinked and forced myself to unclench my fists. Ara wasn't mine, even if every part of me wanted to claim her. Acting this way would only drive her farther away from me.

"Let's go." I followed my sister, ignoring Vanth and Ara, knowing walking away was the best way to tamp down the jealousy.

Laera sent floating lights ahead of us, they twinkled and sparkled in the darkness, illuminating the passageway. It was more white marble, cut with uneven strokes. Jagged edges showed where the masons had hacked at it too quickly or without much care.

The feeling of the magic had eased, but the pull was still there, urging us forward.

"Is that a mate thing?" Sophia asked after we'd been walking a while in silence. "The whole 'touch her and you die' thing?"

Laera laughed and I scowled. Now that I'd had some distance, I realized how foolish I'd looked. Vanth wasn't a threat. And Ara didn't want me, anyway.

"That's what's going on between you, isn't it?" She sounded uncertain, like she was testing out a new language.

I hesitated, wondering how much I should say. Traditionally, it was up to each person to share their mating bond with their family. It wasn't my place, but nobody in Athos expected a mating bond in the first place.

"Things between us are complicated," I finally settled on.

"He fucked up, that's what he's trying to say," Laera added. "He had her, but he lost her."

"Love makes us do stupid things," Sophia said.

"Are you actually defending him?" Laera scoffed. "The magic in this tunnel must be getting to your head."

Sophia chuckled. "I've just seen my share of strange behaviors from people who have paired off."

"She's right, I did fuck up," I admitted.

"Ara deserves better than she got, you know," Sophia said. "I know everyone thinks I don't notice what's going on around the palace. That I don't know how much she takes on or what is asked of her. They coddled me, but that meant they didn't worry as much about what they said around me."

"I know she deserves better," I said.

"She's already lost so much. Given up everything she had for everyone else. My greatest hope for her is that she can find a way to live for herself instead of everyone else," Sophia said.

"I know. She deserves to be happy," I agreed.

"She deserves someone who won't give up on her," Sophia clarified.

I straightened, and a little flicker of hope ignited in my chest. Was she saying what I thought she was saying?

"If you think you can give her that, you should fight for her. But if you hurt her, I'll tear your throat out," Sophia said.

Laera cackled. "And everyone thought you were the sweet, innocent sister."

I shook my head. If we got through this, I would live the rest of my life trying to be the man Ara deserved. I'd make it up to her and I wouldn't stop trying until the day I stopped breathing.

The floor rumbled and I stopped walking. "Did you feel that?"

Laera had her weapons ready. "Stay behind me, Sophia."

I moved closer to the princess, sandwiching her between us. "Be ready to run if needed."

The ground shook again, vibrating the entire cave. Small pieces of marble and dust rained down on us, making us cough. The rumbling intensified. Something was definitely coming for us, but I couldn't tell from which direction. "Where is it?"

"I don't know," Laera sounded stressed, a rare occurrence from her. She was usually very good at masking her emotions.

I gripped my sword, ready to strike whenever the creature revealed itself. More shaking, more falling chunks of marble, more dust.

I took a step forward, back toward the way we'd come. I could feel something nearing and I was pretty sure it had chased us into this chamber from another passage behind the closed door. Whatever this was, it had been here a long time, trapped in this magical vault. And it was angry.

The scent of decay and salt filled my nostrils, and I heard Sophia gagging behind me. Laera made a disgusted whine.

Then the monster turned the corner and we saw the serpentine head leading the long, slithering body as it charged us, undulating and writhing as it made its way down the cave.

I could feel it, the pulsing life of it, the heavy breathing, the fear that drove it. "Laera, can you get a read on it?"

"No, just kill it," she shouted.

I lowered my sword then held up my other hand, the power flowing through me without warning. Ara's power. Ceto's power.

The beast slowed, but the fear still lingered. It snapped its jaws, moving its large golden eyes around the space, taking us all in. I felt hunger. An ache that nearly made me double over from the pain. Wincing, I took a step forward, trying to force down the feeling.

The beast stopped, its large pale green head moving from side to side while its long shimmery body stayed still. It hissed, a blue tongue darting out while it continued its sideways undulation.

Ara's magic flared inside me, demanding use. I leaned into it, hoping she'd forgive me for letting it flow, for using it after I'd sworn not to.

I closed my eyes and visualized the tunnels, imagining the path we'd taken, showing the way through the Opal, out into the streets, toward the sea. I pictured fish and sea life swimming freely, a welcome meal for a hungry monster.

The snake hissed again and I opened my eyes, tightening my grip on my sword.

To my surprise, it backed away, and I could sense its interest in the message I'd sent. It turned, heading the way we'd come, toward the door. The massive tail slammed into the walls as it went, continuing the vibrations. I had to cover my head to keep from being pelted by the falling debris. When I looked up, it was out of sight.

"Whatever you did, well done," Laera said.

"Is it gone?" Sophia asked. "Are there more?"

Suddenly, I heard a scream. A voice I'd know anywhere.

Ara.

I'd sent the beast right for her.

I ran and found myself facing the door we'd opened from the other side. It had closed behind us. "Ara!" I pounded on the door, then looked around, desperate to find a way to open it.

"Help me get this open!" I yelled to Laera and Sophia.

That's when the ground vibrated again and I looked over to see hundreds of spiders the size of horses racing toward us.

"Run!" Laera screamed. "If we don't run now, you're going to die before you see Ara again!"

I gave one last look at the door, then ran.

22

ARA

VANTH WAS HOLDING my hair while I continued to empty my stomach. My forehead was damp with sweat and the world still spun. Though, it wasn't as bad as it had been.

Finally, I stood and wiped my mouth with the back of my hand. Vanth released his grip on my hair. I glanced at him, waiting for him to say something judgmental, but he was just looking at me like I was made of glass. That was even worse.

I glanced down the hall toward the door that led to the magic. I could still feel it lingering, but it wasn't as intense as it had been. Vanth had just enough time to explain that I'd passed out before I got sick.

"Better?" Vanth asked.

I used my sleeves to wipe the sweat from my brow, then nodded. The dizziness had faded, and I was regaining control of my breathing. Plus, I didn't feel like I needed to vomit anymore, so that seemed like a minor victory.

"We should go back," I said.

Vanth lifted a skeptical brow.

"It's probably dissipated by now." I wasn't sure if I was trying to convince him or myself.

The ground rumbled and dust and debris fell from the ceiling. I shielded my eyes as I worked to maintain my balance, hoping the shaking would cease. Instead, it intensified. "What is that?"

"I don't know." Vanth drew his sword.

I pulled my daggers from their sheaths at my hips and turned toward the door we'd just come through. "Something is coming."

Vanth moved in front of me, then glanced behind us. "We should run."

A massive serpent's head emerged through the door and any thoughts of fleeing were erased. The creature charged forward, its body whipping back and forth in undulating movements as it came through the darkness.

Its sickly green scales had a dull sheen to them, nothing like the beautiful opalescent gleam I'd seen on the serpent in the sea. It hissed, showing fangs and a forked blue tongue.

"Vanth..." I moved next to him, my weapons raised.

"On my count, we go for the throat. Avoid its jaws, it could have venom," he called.

Everything was moving too quickly and too slowly at the same time. Waiting for the creature to reach us felt like an eternity, even though I knew it was only a few heartbeats.

Gripping my daggers tighter against my sweaty palms, I tensed, preparing to attack.

The monster's huge tail slammed into the sliding door as it passed through, making the whole tunnel shake violently.

Huge chunks of marble fell around us, and I coughed away the dust, blinking rapidly to keep the falling debris from my eyes without having to turn my focus away from the creature.

"Now," Vanth yelled.

We both charged forward. The shifter went left, leaping into the air and landing on top of the serpent. I went right and without hesitating, dug my dagger deep into the scaly flesh. I cut through the tough skin, grunting as I pulled my dagger. Dark black blood oozed from the injury, accompanied by a stench that reminded me all too closely of rotting animals. I was grateful there was nothing left in my stomach to spill and tried to avoid breathing through my nose as I dug my other blade into the monster.

The creature howled, a sound that made my bones vibrate and set my teeth on edge. I sliced upward, but my daggers weren't doing anything other than angering the beast.

"Look out," Vanth cried.

I tugged my dagger free as the shifter leaped from the bleeding serpent to the ground next to me. The giant head turned to us, hissing and sending spittle and blood spraying all over us. I gagged, then wiped my eyes as quickly as I could.

"Run!" Vanth yelled as he grabbed my arm. We slipped past the serpent, heading toward the entrance we'd come in. I could hear the creature following us. It moved fast, the injuries hardly slowing it down.

It snapped its jaws, but I didn't look back, aiming for the way out. Suddenly, I heard a snarl, and I glanced to my side, seeing a massive wolf where Vanth had been. He charged for the monster, teeth bared, claws extended.

The serpent stopped its progress and reared its massive

head, showing its teeth to the oncoming wolf. Vanth leaped, landing on the monster, digging his claws into its side then sliding down.

The snake howled, screaming so sharply I winced. Then it whipped its neck, sending Vanth to the ground. He landed hard.

"Vanth!" I ran toward my friend, but the snake moved too fast, cutting me off from him and forming a barrier around the fallen shifter.

Vanth's wolf rose, but the snake wrapped its long tail around him, capturing him. The wolf bit and growled and struggled, but despite the fresh wounds and oozing blood, the serpent seemed undeterred.

I noticed Vanth's abandoned sword on the ground. I couldn't hold it long, but I didn't need long. I just needed a little bit of luck. Saying a quick prayer to any of the gods who might still be on my side, more out of habit than anything else, I charged.

The snake opened its mouth, hissing and snapping its jaw. It didn't strike, it was waiting for me. I smiled as I ran toward it, knowing it was underestimating me.

Gripping the sword with everything I had, I aimed it upward just as I reached the monster. It struck, and I stabbed the beast through its mouth, upward into its head. Using everything I had, I pushed the sword. One of the monstrous fangs caught my arm, slicing deep. I cried out, the pain making me lose my grip.

Stumbling backward, I grabbed one of my daggers with my good hand, letting my injured arm hang by my side.

The monster flailed, whipping its head from side to side, smacking the sides of the tunnel as it blindly struggled with the sword lodged in it. More debris and dust fell, and I stepped back more, avoiding the creature as it cried in agony.

Finally, the beast collapsed, making a few last gurgling sounds as its gold eyes went eerily blank.

The massive body went slack, and Vanth clawed his way out of the hold, shaking his head once he was free.

"Are you alright?" I asked the wolf.

He shivered, then his body began to crack and break. I turned away, not wanting to watch as he left one form to return to the other.

I heard him gathering the torn clothing on the ground and gave him a moment before I turned to him. He had his tunic on but was holding it together like a robe. It barely covered him. I scanned him for injuries and saw a few scrapes, the crimson of his blood standing out against the white marble dust he was covered in.

"You seem alright," I said, relieved.

He walked over to me and touched the skin under the slice on my arm. "Is that from the fangs?"

I winced. "Yeah, but it's not too bad."

"We need to get you to a healer in case it was venomous." He turned back to the fallen monster, then looked at me. "Well done. You didn't even need magic to take that beast down."

I shrugged. "It was nothing."

He chuckled. We both knew I was lying. That serpent had almost killed us both.

"The door closed," I said.

"They'll be alright," Vanth replied.

"What if there's more of these monsters in there?" I asked.

"I imagine there are," he said. "But they'll regret crossing paths with Ryvin and Laera."

I forced a smile, trying not to show how worried I was. Or how badly I wanted to be there with them, helping them. I hated that we were back here while Sophia was helping Ryvin and Laera free the magic. "Do you think they'll be able to do it?"

"I hope so," Vanth said. "Without those dragons, Athos doesn't stand a chance."

The walk back to the palace felt like an eternity, but I refused to let Vanth carry me as he offered so many times. Panting and shaking, I made it to the gates, where the guards quickly let us in. At least they could still recognize me in this state.

As we ascended the stairs toward the entry, a rush of heat, then cold burned through me in a flash so fast I wasn't sure if I imagined it. With a gasp, my eyes widened and I looked around for the source of the sensation.

"I think they released the magic," Vanth said.

Shoulders easing in relief, I let out a breath. "At least something went right."

"Ara?" Lagina's tone was panicked. "What happened? Where are the others?"

My sister was running down the stairs, Argus and the Dragon King following in her wake.

"I'm fine," I said, knowing I wasn't fine. But I was alive, and that was about as good as I could hope for anymore.

"Let me help you." She wrapped her arm around my waist. "Someone, call a healer. Find the best one you can. Someone discrete."

"They'll all be at the temples," Istvan's slimy tone said. "I can help."

"I'll take my chances on my own, thanks," I replied.

"Ara don't be foolish. Your entire arm is covered in blood," Lagina scolded.

"Find someone else," I hissed.

"If I was going to harm you, I'd have done it a long time ago, Princess," Istvan said.

I noticed Vanth nearby and reached out for him, pulling him to me even as my sister pushed me closer to the entry. "Don't let him near me."

The shifter nodded. "I'm responsible for her. You can return to your other duties."

"Ara—" Lagina's tone was preparing for a lecture, but I wasn't going to let her start.

"I'm fine, Gina. Really." I glanced at the Dragon King. "Shouldn't you be testing your shifting? See if it works yet?"

"Is it done?" Lagina asked. "Did it work?"

"Only one way to find out," I replied, keeping my attention on the king.

23

We were followed by the skittering sounds of hundreds of legs clicking over the marble. I'd never seen monsters like this, and I could die happy never seeing them again. Spiders hadn't bothered me before, though they were one of Laera's few fears. But these things made my skin crawl. Calling my shadows, I sent them behind us, snuffing out the lights Laera had created and swallowing the spiders chasing us.

I could still hear them, skittering along the marble in the darkness. I summoned shadows from the depths of my magic, sending them swirling around the monsters. Squeezing them with darkness, trying to smother the creatures. They continued as if my magic was nothing.

"My magic doesn't work on them," I called through the darkness.

"Of course it doesn't," Laera gritted out. She ignited the

lights again and I rushed ahead, catching up to her and Sophia.

"Do something!" Sophia yelled, her tone pure panic.

I glanced over my shoulder to see the creatures gaining on us. We were lucky they didn't move too quickly. I got the distinct impression they were corralling us, chasing but not attacking.

"We must be nearing a dead end," I said.

"Kill them, Ryvin," Laera snapped. "That's what you do. You kill things. Kill them."

My stomach tightened. It was what I did. What I was known for. But my shadows had failed. I stopped and turned, pulling my sword from its holster and facing the spiders. "Keep going! Do what needs to be done!"

I tightened my grip, ready to slice down as many of these things as I could. If nothing else, I could give them a chance to free the rest of the magic.

"Don't die, Ryvin. I won't be able to keep the gods away from Ara," Laera said.

I cursed. She was right. This would not be my last stand. I would prevail. Hating myself, I called to the unfamiliar magic in my veins that I'd already tapped into once. That swimming, tangled mess that didn't belong to me. It resisted at first, as if it knew I'd violated my promise when I'd used it against the serpent.

Reaching out toward the spiders, I sent whatever I could grasp. The magic opened, responding to the creatures rather than to me. It was as if it recognized the presence of monsters, ignoring the fact that a stranger was wielding it.

"Stop!" I yelled, sending every bit of Ara's magic I could summon toward the massive creatures.

They slowed, moving cautiously now.

I pushed again, this time adding my own magic to the mix. Shadows moved in swirling tendrils, winding their way around the spiders, wrapping around legs and bodies, holding them in place. It was enough to get them to stop moving, but I could sense their hunger; their desire to destroy all of us.

These caves were their home, and we were a threat.

"We aren't going to hurt you." I felt ridiculous speaking to them and had no way of knowing if they could understand.

They started moving again, fighting against the shadows, pushing through. Clicking and hissing, the creatures struggled against the bonds.

They wanted me dead.

I wasn't sure how I knew, but I could tell they were not going to stop until they feasted on all of us. Fuck.

"Laera, whatever you're doing, move faster," I yelled. One by one, the creatures freed themselves from my shadows. Bit by bit, they moved closer to me. Beady eyes gleamed in lights left behind by Laera. Their legs clicked against the marble ground as they moved in unison.

I raised my sword and I charged.

One at a time, I struck down the spiders. They surrounded me, clicking and skittering and grabbling. I cut off legs and heads and dug my sword into their bodies.

Sweat dripped down my face as I sent shadows to hold back as many as I could while I fought the closest threat. They seemed to be getting faster at breaking through my magic, attacking in groups. Jaws snapped; fangs glistened. I managed to avoid their teeth, not knowing if they were venomous.

The bodies piled up, legs sticking out in every direction. I climbed on top of fallen spiders to reach those I'd been holding back. As soon as they broke free of my shadows, I charged them, taking them out little by little until I was left panting in a sea of fallen creatures.

Legs twitched and blank eyes stared at me. While I caught my breath, I looked around at the slaughter, making sure they were all dead.

I was covered in dark, sticky blood and most of my magic had been depleted from keeping them at bay. How had they resisted me? I'd taken down whole battlefields, but these spiders had only found my magic a hindrance for a short time. It was as if they'd fed on my magic, draining it from me as I used it.

Shaking my head, I climbed down the mountain of spiders, still gripping my sword. I had to find Laera. Whatever magic had been trapped down here must have impacted the creatures that dwelled here. That must have been how they fought off my magic.

I didn't want to run into anything else. We had to find the rest of the trapped magic and get out of here before we ended up as a meal for something worse than the spiders.

"They're dead, right?" Laera said when she heard me approach. She didn't even take her eyes off the huge circular door she was staring at. I could feel the magic pulsing like the heat of a fire trapped behind a wall. It wanted out.

"They're dead," I said. "But they resisted my magic. If we run into anything else down here, we could be in trouble."

Laera glanced over her shoulder. "Then let's do this and get out of here before anything else can find us."

"We don't know how to open it," Sophia said. She was

pale and trembling. I wasn't even sure how she was still functioning after everything she'd seen. Ara was right, she was stronger than we realized.

Blood dripped from her hand, and I noticed there was a crimson smear on the door. Apparently, that wasn't the way to open this.

I approached and set my palm against the cool marble. Unlike the harshly carved walls, this was smooth and polished. Whoever had made this had put care into it.

I set my other hand against it and the magic flared, sending a rush through me that made me gasp.

"What did you do?" Laera demanded.

"Nothing. I just touched it," I said.

She pressed her palms against it and nothing happened. "Sophia, touch the wall. See if anything reacts."

The princess put both of her hands against the marble surface. We got a smaller pulse of magic, but it was something.

I lifted a brow and looked over at Laera. She stepped away from the door and I followed, moving backward so I could take the whole thing in better. "It can't be tied to blood if it reacted to you. Is it responding to magic? It didn't recognize mine."

"It's recognizing Ara's." It was absurd. Ara never knew she had this power. How had her father designed something like this with her magic as part of the key?

"Try it," Sophia stepped back from the door. "Use her magic. See if that makes it open."

I nodded, then took a deep breath, tapping into that magic again. Pushing past the guilt, I fought for it, calling it forward. It came easier this time, even without a creature to respond to. I wasn't sure if that was a good thing or a bad thing.

Ara was never going to speak to me again when she found out how much I'd used her magic.

The door shuddered, then stilled. No rush of magic, no sign that it was responding to what I'd sent.

"It's not the magic," Laera sounded surprised.

Sophia moved closer, touching it again. The little trickle of magic seemed to be radiating from the door, making the tunnel around us shimmer.

I touched it again, getting an even greater reaction. It ignored Laera, not responding at all to her touch. She stepped away, then shook her head. "You have got to be kidding me."

"What?" I asked.

She scoffed. "It's your fucking bond. It recognizes you as family."

My heart fell into my stomach. I'd heard about how connected a mating bond made someone. Two halves of the same whole. But enough to trigger a family connection on a magically sealed door? "That can't be."

"It is," she said. "You're part of her, even if she doesn't want you."

My insides twisted.

Sophia glanced over at me. "Together, then. Whatever we have." She closed her eyes, and I was impressed by how she went with her instincts.

I cursed under my breath. I didn't feel worthy of using my ties to Ara and her family for this. Until I earned her trust back, until I earned her love back, I felt like a fraud doing this.

"Just do it," Laera ordered.

I gritted my teeth, and I thought about Ara. I thought about the first time I saw her in Athos. How my heart had skipped a beat, how I'd known I had to have her even if I didn't yet know why. How I'd resisted, fought against the connection. I knew I was wrong for her. I knew she deserved more than me. I'd tried to get her out of my system with other women. I'd tried so fucking hard to not want her. But she was the only one I wanted. I craved her. She was the air I breathed, the water I drank; she was everything that made life worth living. Without her, there was nothing but darkness.

Shadows rose up around us of their own accord, my emotions sending them swirling and churning.

"Ryvin..." Laera warned.

The ground shook and magic swelled around me.

"Don't stop!" Sophia shouted.

Blood was pouring from her nose, and I could feel my shadows tangling with the magic surrounding us. Wind roared, whipping my hair around my face. My ears hurt as pressure built in my head.

"The door's moving," Laera shouted. "Keep going!"

The ground shook, vibrating as the massive marble slab rolled aside. I kept my hands steady, letting the door move under them. As it shifted, I was left standing in a void, the door no longer under my palms. I stumbled, struggling to remain upright as a wild and turbulent wind laced with magic rushed past. I could taste lightning and my skin tingled so much it made me wince in pain. Sophia collapsed, but Laera was there to catch her before she hit the ground.

I dropped to my knees, using the ground to brace myself

as the onslaught of power continued to pummel us as it flowed from the opening. The world spun and nausea rolled through me. Just as I thought I might pass out, the wind died down and we were left with the glistening remains of magic hanging around us. Blue shimmers sparkled in the air, floating like tiny jewels.

I stood, moving my hand through the air, touching the floating particles and feeling a little jolt from each one I touched. We did it. Dropping my arm, I let out a long breath and my shoulders sagged.

"I hope that was enough for the dragons because I am not doing that again," Laera said.

I laughed, feeling a little insane after everything we'd just experienced.

She stood, lifting the still unconscious princess with her. I went to her side and took Sophia from her, holding her in my arms the same way Vanth had carried Ara out of here.

"Those Athos princesses sure like the drama," Laera said.

"They're both half human. I'm impressed they lasted as long as they did," I said as we made our way back out of the tunnel.

"Ara might be full human now," Laera replied.

I thought about the shadows she'd called from me and how I'd been able to tap into her magic. She wasn't as weak as my sister thought she was. Everyone was going to underestimate her. And I couldn't help but think there was a way to use that to our advantage. I just wasn't sure how yet.

Laera froze, sucking in a breath as her gaze went blank. I stopped moving. She was seeing something.

A moment later she shook her head, then her eyes found mine again, refocusing on the present.

"What is it?" I asked.

"They all joined him. All of them. Even the Gold Court and the Mountain Dwellers. We're on our own." She huffed out a breath that sounded like defeat. "The ships from Telos are on their way to Konos for final orders."

"How much time?" I asked.

"They'll arrive in two days, and they aren't going to take any prisoners," she said.

24

ARA

WATCHING the king twist and break and contort was too much. I winced and turned away, unable to stomach seeing his human form endure the pain the change caused. I'd seen Vanth go through the same thing, but I wasn't ever going to get used to it and avoided watching when possible.

"Gods help us," Vanth murmured next to me.

I looked back to see a massive dragon rising from the ground. Huge wings spread wide, sending gusts of wind that blew my hair in front of my face as it climbed into the sky.

Midnight blue scales glinted in the torchlights, the beast blending more with the night sky with each passing wing-beat. He was amazing. Terrifying and beautiful all at once. Nearly a perfect match with the night sky.

"I'm supposed to marry that," Cora said quietly.

I hadn't even heard her join us. I turned to see her staring up at the Dragon King in horror. All color gone.

"He's a monster," she whispered.

I looked back at the massive dragon flying above the palace. His tail whipped behind him, tipped with dangerous looking spikes. Huge claws glinted on his arms and legs. I knew sharp teeth resided within the beast's massive jaw.

"We'll figure something out." Between Lagina promising Cora and the bond, I wasn't sure what was going to happen, and I didn't know what to say.

Cora clasped my hand, moving closer to me. "He won't leave without me."

I squeezed her hand. "Try not to think about that. We have to survive the fae attack first."

He flew past us, going toward the sea until he vanished from sight. I narrowed my eyes, trying to find the creature, but he was hidden by the darkness.

Suddenly, a burst of light erupted, illuminating the dragon against the night sky.

Fire.

He was breathing fire.

My blood ran cold.

I'd trained to fight these creatures. I knew what they were capable of, but seeing one up close showed just how deadly they were.

Cora released my hand and walked away. I lingered for a moment, watching the bursts of flames arcing across the sky before following her. "Wait up," I called.

She turned. "Ara, I love you, I do. But right now, I could use a few minutes alone."

I stilled, watching her walk away and wishing I had the words to help her with this. We needed the Dragon King's help, but I hated that it was all tied to my sister's hand.

"No matter how many times you see it, it's always impressive," Vanth said as he hurried to catch up to me.

"You've fought them before, right? Can they really help us against the fae?" I asked. I needed to know it was worth it.

"Without them, you don't stand a chance," he replied.

"That's not an answer," I said.

"I know."

I didn't push. I had to believe we could do this. Otherwise, what was the point? The lights in the temples still flickered and glowed. I wondered how many people were still there, sitting vigil and praying to the gods.

I couldn't help but imagine the gods surrounded by luxury, watching with amusement as we prepared to destroy each other. Frowning, I picked up the pace. I had always wondered if the gods were real, but now that I'd met some of them, I wished I still didn't know. It was worse knowing they existed, but didn't care. Worse, they might even be enjoying watching us struggle.

As I crossed back into the palace, I heard some commotion. Guards shouted, weapons clattered along the floor. With a glance at Vanth, we came to a silent agreement. We ran toward the sound.

"I don't want to hurt you," a male voice said with a growl.

I picked up the pace, knowing him anywhere. "He's a friend!" I called to the guards without even seeing Ryvin. When I reached them, I slid across the marble floor, throwing my hands out for balance.

The guards looked at me as if they'd never seen anything less dignified. My cheeks heated. "Dust on my sandals." I shook my head. "Never mind. Just let them in. They're with me."

Several of the guards scanned me from head to toe, as if wondering who I was. I was covered in dust and blood. I turned back to Ryvin and noticed that he was holding someone in his arms. "Sophia!"

I bypassed the guards, launching at the prince. "What's wrong with her? What happened?"

"She's alright. Just needs some rest, I think," Ryvin said. His arms were trembling. Sophia's weight was getting to him. I'd never seen him show any signs of weakness. "Are you alright?"

"What's going on here?" Another male voice called.

"Sir," the guards chanted.

I spared a glance to see Argus approaching. "Thank the gods," I breathed out. "Argus, can you take Sophia to her room?"

"The princess?" One of the other guards asked.

"Two princesses, you fool," Argus snapped.

"And the queen," Laera added, joining us.

The guards dropped into a bow.

"Enough ceremony. Someone help Sophia," I ordered.

Argus took my sister from Ryvin and the prince immediately moved to my side. "What happened to your arm?"

"She keeps refusing treatment," Lagina grumbled.

I ignored my sister, looking from Ryvin to Laera and back again. "Are the two of you alright?"

"We're fine," Laera said.

"We saw the dragon fire," Ryvin said.

"He shifted," I confirmed.

"Good." Ryvin ran a hand through his hair and dust and little pebbles fell around him. He avoided looking at me, his gaze darting everywhere else.

"What's wrong?" I could tell he was hiding something.

Laera sighed, the sound exaggerated and heavy. "The Fae King will be here in two days."

"I'll inform the Dragon King. You three get cleaned up and get some rest. We'll catch you up when you're ready." Lagina didn't wait for a response before turning to leave.

The guards around us shifted and fiddled with the weapons by their sides. They all looked so young and untested. I could feel their concern, but I didn't have any comforting words for them.

Ryvin brushed his fingers against my arm, and I hissed. "What are you doing?"

"That needs cleaning at the very least. You should have Vanth take care of it for you." He took a step away. "Get some rest, Ara."

Something deep inside me shattered as he walked away. I wanted to chase him down and drag him to my room with me. I wanted to feel him against me. I wanted to listen to him breathing softly, asleep in the bed next to me.

"Come on," Vanth said. "I'll help you get cleaned up."

"What did I do?" I asked.

"I think he's trying to follow your wishes," Vanth replied.

I swallowed hard. That was what I'd asked for, wasn't it? Why did it hurt so much every time I was away from him? *Stupid mating bond.* It had to be the fault of that bond. I knew he wasn't good for me. I knew I was better off without him. Wasn't I?

We fell into step down the dimly lit halls. Candles let off tendrils of black smoke as they flickered in the night breeze. I peered through the colonnades out toward the sea. Even with the stars, I couldn't tell where the water ended and the sky began. I shivered. It made everything look so much more dangerous.

My room was lit with glowing fae orbs, and I was pretty sure Laera or Ryvin had stopped by to add them for me. My life had turned out so differently from what I expected. Instead of defending Athos's borders against the dragons, I was joining forces with them against the fae.

Vanth turned on the faucet and water ran into the tub. I tensed as I stared at the vessel that had almost cost me my life. I could no longer control water and I waited for the fear to return. It didn't. Cautiously, I moved closer, lowering my fingertips into the stream. It was warm and comforting. I wasn't sure if the fear was gone because I'd reached a level of macabre acceptance about the things I couldn't control or if it was because Vanth made me feel safer.

He untied the makeshift bandage he'd applied in the cave, and I winced as he pulled the fabric away from the sticky blood. The wound looked terrible. It was deep and still oozing. Not to mention the fact that it was coated in dirt and dust.

The shifter found a cloth and a bar of soap and, after wetting it, worked it into a lather. He turned off the water. "I'll help you scrub this out, then you can do the rest."

"Such a gentleman," I teased.

"I'm already risking my life by touching you. You'll want to wash off my scent before you see your mate again," Vanth warned.

I resisted the urge to roll my eyes and opened my mouth to say something snarky when the cloth touched the wound on my arm. I yelped, then pulled my arm away reflexively.

"Stay still," Vanth ordered.

Grumbling, I returned my arm, then took a deep breath. The shifter gently cleaned my arm, alternating between rinsing the cloth in the tub and washing more layers of dust and caked on blood.

I bit down on the inside of my cheek and counted the tiles on the washroom floor to distract myself from the pain. Finally, he tossed the cloth into the murky, red water.

"I think we got lucky," he said, his fingers brushing against the raw skin of my arm. "I don't see any signs of venom or infection."

"Well, that's good," I agreed.

"You are going to have a scar, though. It's too deep and we don't have any magic healers to seal it up in time," he apologized.

"It's alright. I don't mind the scars." My mind instantly showed me the scars on Ryvin's back and I shoved the thought away.

He removed his hand from my arm. "You should clean up. I'll wait in your room until you're finished so I can re-bandage it for you."

"You can go to your room to bathe," I suggested. "I'm fine here."

He gave me an indulgent grin. As if I was a child who'd said something especially amusing. "I'll wait in your room."

I knew I wasn't going to win this argument, so I started taking off my clothes. "As you wish."

His eyes widened and he spun around, his ears bright pink as he hustled out of the bathroom. "Very funny, Ara."

"You wouldn't have to risk seeing me naked if you went to your own room," I reminded him.

"Take your bath, Princess," he called.

I chuckled to myself as I drained and refilled the water. While it was running, I added some of the almond oil that Mila had used for special occasions. With the possibility of every bath being my last, I figured she'd encourage me to use the good stuff. My throat stung as I recalled all the time I'd spent with her and all the time I'd wasted with her.

I should have asked her about her family more often. I should have done kind things for her to make her life better. I missed her so much. I hoped she would be proud of me for the choices I was making now, even if I was learning too late to help her.

The water wasn't as deep as I used to make it, but it was enough to cover my legs. Progress. Climbing inside, I used a new cloth to scrub all the dirt and dust from the caves. I had to add more water so I could rinse my hair, but I didn't stay in the tub long. Vanth deserved his turn to get cleaned up, and I knew he wasn't about to leave my room until I was finished.

I dried quickly and pulled my robe around me before returning to my room. I froze when Ryvin rose from the chair at my desk. He had washed and changed into a casual blue tunic. I'd never seen him in the color of Athos, and I had to admit, it was a good color on him. It conjured memories of the dream I'd had, and warmth pooled between my legs.

"I thought you wanted Vanth to help me." I hated how accusatory my tone came out.

"I can call him back if that's what you'd prefer," he said.

I sighed. "You know that's not what I meant."

He held up a bundle of clean, white bandages. "May I?"

I noticed the sleeve of my robe was already red from the bleeding injury. It needed care. Reluctantly, I turned so I wasn't facing him, then pulled my arm out of my robe, then gathered the fabric to cover my chest before facing him.

He was gentle as he wrapped the strips of fabric around my arm, his touch soft and steady. I breathed in his scent and closed my eyes, forcing myself to think about anything other than him in my bed.

When he finished, he stepped back, leaving a large space between us. I tensed. Was he feeling the same thing as me, or was he no longer interested in me?

"I came to talk to you." He shifted uncomfortably.

My brow furrowed. He ran a hand through his hair and looked down at the floor.

"You're nervous." My heart raced. "What's wrong? Is it one of my sisters? Did something happen?"

His eyes widened. "No, nothing like that. Just, I want you to trust me again. Someday. So I need to tell you something."

My first thought was that he'd been with another woman, but I had to remind myself that we weren't together anymore. And also, that there'd been no time for that. How would he have even met someone to hook up with in the first place?

Annoyed at myself for getting jealous so easily, I crossed my arms over my chest and waited.

"I used your magic," he confessed.

I dropped my arms to my sides. I hadn't expected him to say that, and I had no idea how to react.

"Vanth told me what happened with the serpent and it's my fault. I used your magic on it and accidentally sent it to you and I am so sorry," he admitted.

"That monster came after me because of you?" My voice came out too high.

"Not on purpose. I sent it away from us, but it ended up

running into you and Vanth and if you hadn't stopped it..." He shook his head. "That injury you have, that's because of me."

A strange hollow sensation filled my chest, but it wasn't as empty or angry as it had been. "Without my magic, it could have killed you. And Laera. And Sophia."

"Possibly. I should have just fought it. I don't know why I used your magic. It just reacted. I promised you I wouldn't. It wasn't my intention, I swear," he said.

"Is that it?" I asked.

"No," he replied.

"What else could you possibly have done?" I asked, not sure I wanted to know.

"Well, it's not something I've done yet. It's something I intend to do," he answered.

I lifted a brow in silent question.

"We have two days until my father arrives. I plan to use that time to teach you to use my shadows."

25

ARA

"HE'S GOT ALL the other courts joining him," Laera announced. "Even if they don't want to."

"And it's not possible to deter any of them from joining?" Lagina asked.

Laera shook her head. "As long as he's breathing, they're too afraid of him to stand against him."

"Why?" I asked. "Without Nyx's power and without his monster, he's not what he was. None of them are willing to risk it?"

"He's got something on them," Ryvin added.

"I agree. But I can't see what it is. Somehow, he's blocked me from gaining certain information," Laera confessed.

Ryvin gave her a sideways glance, showing a moment of concern before letting his expression go blank. It was enough to set me even more on edge.

"The rest of my men will be here tomorrow," the Dragon

King said. "With our magic restored, we can attack before the ships even reach the shore."

"Shouldn't that be enough?" Sophia asked. "Can't you just burn them all before they get to us?"

"They'll fight back," Laera said impossibly gently. For everyone else, it was sarcasm and vitriol. But the Fae Princess had a soft spot for Sophia. I supposed it was her gift. Everyone had always treated her that way.

"I still think all of this is a terrible idea," Cora mumbled.

"Did you have something to add, my bride?" the Dragon King asked.

Cora sighed. "Don't call me that."

He shrugged and I caught the little smirk before he shrugged. "As you wish, Princess."

Cora rolled her eyes. "I don't even know why I'm here. You all seem like you've made up your mind about this."

"We don't have a choice, Cora," I said.

"We can run. We've done it before. We could start over somewhere new. If dragons aren't enough to stop the fae from reaching Athos, what chance do we have?" she asked.

"You think they'd let us go? You think they wouldn't chase us? How many of us would survive a week in the Spine?" I asked.

"They want Drakous," Ryvin said. "Us going there will just turn their attention to their ultimate goal quicker. Athos is nothing. It's petty revenge, nothing more. If all the humans left, he'd just focus on Drakous and let all of you die on your way there."

Cora pressed her fingers to her temples. "This is why I don't belong here. None of this even makes sense to me. You need a real council."

Lagina reached out across the table and pulled Cora's arm down so she could clasp her hand. "This is my council. You're an important part of it."

"I don't understand all this," Cora said. "Why do the fae even care?"

"You can't think about the reasons," Lagina said. "Focus on how we can save our kingdom."

Cora nodded, but she didn't look convinced.

"You're the people I trust. None of Father's council was reliable, and I certainly can't trust Istvan," Lagina said.

I glanced toward the door as if I'd see the slimy priest poking his head in. Lagina had sent him to oversee the construction of the new temple to Nyx. They were already digging to clear space for it so we could show the goddess the progress whenever she decided to come here to destroy us.

"You'll learn. This is good practice for you. If you choose to participate, the queen's voice is just as important as the king's in Drakous," the Dragon King said.

Cora tensed, and I felt a little jolt at his words. Of course, I knew that was how it worked, but imagining Cora as a queen was going to take some getting used to.

"Vanth can help prepare your men," Ryvin suggested.

"I can accompany him," the Dragon King offered. "They should get used to seeing a dragon before my men arrive tomorrow."

Lagina nodded. "Good. Let's conclude for now and we'll reconvene tomorrow to share any new information."

Everyone around the table stood and we started toward the door. Argus, who had been silent the whole meeting, escorted Sophia while Cora ducked out without turning back. Vanth and the Dragon King left together, which was an odd pairing, leaving me with Lagina, Ryvin, and Laera.

My sister pulled me aside and whispered, "You trust this information, right? It's still hard to trust anyone from Konos."

"They want the king dead just as much as I do," I replied.

Laera nodded. "Alright." She straightened, then spoke in her normal tone, "I'm going to see about the status of the new temple. I'll see you for dinner?"

"I'll be there," I assured her.

She glanced at Ryvin and Laera before making her way out of the room. I turned to the siblings. "What do you two have planned?"

"None of your business," Laera snapped before flipping her long silver hair over her shoulder, then walked toward the door. "See you later."

I shook my head. At least she was back to acting like her usual self.

"Come on, we've got work to do," Ryvin said.

My stomach twisted into knots. I was nervous about tapping into his shadows, but I had to admit, I was also excited. That little part of me that craved power seemed to purr in anticipation.

LAGINA HATED THE THRONE ROOM, which was probably why it was empty when we arrived. Ryvin closed the door behind us, momentarily sealing us into the darkness before he released several floating fae orbs of light.

"This is really the place you want to work on shadows

with me?" I couldn't help but think about what he'd done with his shadows the last time I'd been in this room with him.

"I know it's not ideal and I know what it reminds you of, but it's warded. Nobody can hear or feel what we're doing in here," he said.

That explained why additional guards didn't run in after Ryvin killed my father. Chills ran down my spine and I had to turn away from the prince to collect myself. How did I reconcile the monster my father had been with the man I thought I knew? And how was I supposed to make any sense of the fact that I was still in love with his killer?

Something was so very wrong with me.

"Would you like me to find another place?" Ryvin asked.

I took a deep breath, then turned to face him. "No. This is fine. Good, even." Because it reminded me of why I couldn't let my feelings dictate my actions with him.

"Very well. We should start with something easy and work our way up. Since I was able to use your magic while we weren't next to each other, I think it might be possible for you to tap into mine even when we're not together. That way, you're never defenseless.

"When you accessed my magic before, your emotions were high, and the danger was great. The first test will be to see if you can summon my power on purpose."

He took a step closer to me, then extended his hand. "Touch might make it easier."

I glanced at his hand and hesitated. My heart pounded and my skin already felt too hot. I wished it was because of the prospect of what I was about to attempt. Or the fact that I was back in the place where this man had killed my own father. But it wasn't. It was the fact that I knew that once I touched him, I was going to have a hard time focusing on what we needed to do.

I took a step back. "I'd rather try without touch. I won't always have you by my side."

He dropped his hand, and I could almost feel the disappointment. "Alright."

"Do you think it's the same as when I used my magic before?" I shoved down the frustration of starting over. With his magic, instead of mine.

"Maybe. Why don't you try what worked for you before? See if you can tap into me."

I opened myself up, mentally feeling for the sensations I'd noticed before. That little dark part of me that I tried to repress flared to life and seemed to reach for Ryvin. I could feel him, not in the way I had before. It was different. Like I was feeling all the things that made him who he was. My body felt light and full of possibilities. There was a connection, a thread, that seemed to span from me to him.

I stepped closer to him, letting my instincts lead, until I was right in front of him. He was shimmering. Blue lights danced in the space between us like bits of fragmented stars.

"What are you doing?" he asked, a little breathless.

"I don't know." I reached for him. As soon as my fingers grazed his cheek, a jolt ran through me. My back arched and pain zigzagged down my spine like a jolt of lightning.

Ryvin grabbed me, catching me before I fell. "What did you do?" He stroked my hair back as he lowered us to the ground.

I blinked up at him. "I have no idea."

Shadows swirled around us, cocooning us in a cylinder of

darkness dotted with hundreds of twinkling blue lights that floated around us like bits of embers.

I sat up, pushing free of his grip as I looked at the cyclone we'd created. "Was that me or you?"

"I think it was us," he said.

I stretched my fingers out, touching the swirling black shadows. Little sparks danced where I touched, making me shiver. I lifted my hand, staring at my palm in disbelief. I wasn't sure what we'd done or how it would help us, but it felt like the start of something greater.

Ryvin reached for me, lining his palm up with mine, then lowered his fingers so he was holding my hand. I clasped my fingers down as well, then stared at our woven grip. The charge around us intensified, and I could feel all the hair on my arms stand on end.

Shadows poured from him, twisting and twining around my arm, circling me like dark ribbons. I gasped in fear, recalling what I'd seen those shadows do when they encased someone. The sensation was short-lived, though, because somehow, I knew they weren't going to harm me.

They were playful, twisting and churning, circling around me like friendly serpents. I giggled, then looked at Ryvin. He was grinning, but I noticed none of the shadows were around him. "Did I take them all?"

He lifted his free arm and flicked his wrist. Nothing happened. He shrugged. "I guess so."

"I can't do that. I can't use your magic if it takes it from you," I said.

He wrapped his free arm around my back, then tugged me closer until my knees were touching his. "I would give it all to you if it meant knowing that you were safe. You have to know that. Take it. Everything I have is yours."

The look in his eyes was pure want. A hungry expression that made my hands tremble. After everything we've been through, he still looked at me as if I was the only person he ever wanted to look at again. And despite myself, I couldn't help but return that gaze, staring into the swirling depths of his silver eyes. There was something else there, too. Exhaustion. Weakness. Pain.

Blood began to drip from his nose.

I let go of his magic abruptly. Tugging my sleeve over my hand, I leaned forward and wiped the blood away. He caught my wrist. "I'm fine."

"You're not fine." I sat back on my heels. "I was hurting you."

"I can handle it," he said.

I shook my head. "No. Your body was fighting back, like you said. It didn't want me to use your magic."

"You weren't just using it," he explained. "You were siphoning it. Taking it...the way I took yours."

For a moment, the darkness flared, anxious for more. I shoved it down. I couldn't do what he'd done to me.

Ryvin took hold of my face, a hand on each cheek. "You need to take it, Ara. All of it. But it can't be when I expect it or my body will fight it."

"I couldn't," I said.

"You can. It's perfect. The gods said you can't have Ceto's magic. They never said you can't have mine." He was smiling, but I could hear the shallowness of his breathing. The short time I'd siphoned his magic had cost him.

"I won't," I said.

"You have to. It's the only way to keep you safe. The only way I can begin to make amends for what I did." He stroked his thumb along my cheekbone. "Please, Ara. I need you to live. You have to know that."

"Stop asking me to take your magic," I said.

He opened his mouth to speak, but I leaned forward and pressed my lips to his, silencing his protests.

26

ARA

HE KISSED ME BACK, hungry and desperate. His hands were in my hair and mine slid down his back, pulling him closer to me. I needed this. I needed him.

Our tongues battled and my fingers dug into him, grabbing hold as if I'd lose him if I released him. The kiss was everything I was, and I could feel how much of himself he was giving me as our lips and tongues clashed.

Magic flared, shadows and cold swirling around us like a storm. My skin tingled and it felt like lightning shot down my spine.

My hair whipped around my face and I held on tight, relishing the feel of our bodies connected, pressed together so close it was impossible to know where he ended and I began.

Then I tasted copper and I gasped, breaking free of his kiss. He grabbed my tunic and pulled me back to him, but I resisted, using my thumb to wipe the blood from under his nose.

The shadows around us dissipated and the wind settled. We'd created that without trying. Our emotions had summoned magic that was harming him. Or I had tried to siphon more of his while we kissed.

"Don't stop," he whispered.

I held up my fingers, showing the bright crimson. "We can't do this. Look what it's doing to you."

"I'm fine." He wiped his nose with his sleeve.

I stood, then extended my hand, offering to help him up. He raised a brow, as if getting help from me was insulting. I rolled my eyes. "I nearly took all your magic. Trust me, I know how exhausting that is."

He sighed, then accepted my hand, but he didn't actually pull on me at all as he rose. I felt a little better knowing he was at least strong enough to get himself up, and I hoped I hadn't caused any injuries that he wouldn't recover from.

We were dealing with things beyond our knowledge. "You said before that mates can share magic. How do we do that without me taking?"

"I thought that's what we were doing, but I guess not," he said.

"If this is to help me defend myself, we should practice that." I started walking toward the door, then looked over my shoulder. "Unless you need time to rest?"

"What do you have in mind?" He followed me, stopping next to me by the door.

"We fight. Train with weapons, add in some magic while we do it," I said. "That's more realistic anyway, isn't it? I won't be able to stand in the distance and use my magic against anyone attacking. For me, it would be up close."

I hated that I couldn't be more useful. "You'll have to learn how to control water, maybe even summon some creatures." I swallowed over the lump in my throat. "The gods never said you couldn't use that magic."

"I don't want to use your magic. It was wrong of me to do so before."

"No, don't do that. If it gives us a chance to save my kingdom, we use whatever we have." I opened the door. "Training grounds. Help me borrow just enough of your magic to give me the edge I need to fight against a fae."

"I'm making this up as I go," he said.

"I'm not asking you to be perfect. Just be honest with me." My chest tightened as I walked forward. I resisted the urge to look back to see his reaction. "Tell me if I'm taking too much. Don't hide things from me."

He was so quiet I almost looked back, but I was afraid of what I'd see. I needed honesty from him and I didn't want any expressions of pity.

"Agreed," he finally said.

I let out a slow breath, careful not to let my posture change too much. I didn't want him to know exactly how important this was to me. Because there was a flicker of hope rising. If I could trust him again, would there be a chance for us?

It seemed too big to consider with everything else going on, but staying away from him was more difficult than I thought it would be.

We reached the training grounds to find Vanth and the Dragon King working with a group of guards. They all turned to look at us as we approached. I walked toward the practice swords and grabbed two. There were knives tucked into the holsters on my thighs, so I didn't need more of those.

"This way." I lifted my chin toward a door on the other side of the training grounds.

"What are you all staring at?" Vanth called. "Back to work."

Ryvin followed me into the door without comment. We walked down a long, rarely used hallway toward a room I hadn't been in since I was very young. Ryvin ignited some lights, the floating orbs following us as we made our way through the empty hall.

"I haven't visited this part of the palace," Ryvin said.

I stopped in front of a large, heavy door. "When I was young, we had lessons together in here, but as we got older, the lessons stopped."

I pushed open the door and glanced around the abandoned music room. Cloth covered the largest harp, but the smaller ones and the lyres hanging against the wall were covered in thick dust. Music wasn't a priority for my father or Ophelia, and I'd never had a feel for it, even if I enjoyed listening to others perform.

My feet slid on the dusty marble floor. The servants hadn't even been in here to clean in a long while. "I don't think anyone even remembers about this place. We shouldn't be bothered."

"Good." Ryvin took hold of one of the practice swords I was still carrying. "Show me what you got."

I gripped the sword, then attacked as I'd learned. Ryvin defended, striking with ease. I could tell he was holding back, but I went through the motions anyway, trying to feel for his magic as we sparred.

Tendrils of shadows dusted the floor, wisps of darkness that dissipated like fog as soon as we disturbed it. I knew the magic was there, I could feel it, but every time I caught the thread, Ryvin attacked and I lost focus.

Sweat rolled down my cheek and I was already breathing heavy. The sword had never been my forte and we'd been fighting for a while, our movements almost like a dance. He seemed to have learned the same fighting patterns I did.

Finally, I took a step back, catching my breath. I lowered the weapon. "You're going too easy on me."

"Yet you haven't been able to get any of my magic," he observed.

I pressed my lips together as disappointment made my shoulders sink. My fighting was weaker than his and I couldn't get at the magic to give myself an advantage.

His brow furrowed.

"What?" I asked, knowing he was holding something back.

"I've never seen you use a sword before. Is that what you were trained on?"

"I trained on everything, but I avoid the sword if I can," I admitted. "I know it's harder for me."

"Then why are we using it?" he asked.

"Because that's often what I find in a fight." I shrugged.

"You have knives strapped on you." His eyes dropped to where the knives were strapped to my thighs.

I shivered, then sent away the dirty thoughts that flooded my mind about him and my thighs.

He looked back up at me and smirked.

"Don't give me that look." I tossed the practice sword aside and yanked one of the knives from its holster. Thankfully, I was in a tunic and leggings today. If I'd been in a peplos, I'd have shown off a lot of skin to access this.

Ryvin moved so fast I hardly had time to adjust my grip. I blocked his first strike, the knife vibrating so hard against the practice blade of his sword that it made my teeth chatter.

Ducking low, I broke away from him and spun, striking with my knife. The tip grazed him, but he moved so quickly, he was never at risk of actual injury.

Suddenly, his foot was under mine and I went down, losing my knife as I fell. I crawled, reaching for the blade, but his foot stepped on it, preventing me from grabbing it. I rolled to the other side and quickly got to my feet, pulling my second knife from its holster. Moving fast, I feigned going right, then changed directions, hoping to catch him off guard.

For a moment, I thought I had him. Then the shadows rose, gripping my wrists and tugged my arms to my sides. "You're cheating."

"I'm doing what you're supposed to be doing. Channel it to you, make the shadows work for you," he snapped.

I grunted as I tried to break free of the grip the swirling dark tendrils had on my wrists. Ryvin casually walked toward me, then plucked the knife from my clasped hand, tossing it aside. He leaned closer. "Fight me."

I reached for him, trying to take the shadows with me, looking for that thread that connected us; trying to find that darkness inside me. Of course, it wasn't there when I actually needed it.

Ryvin was right in front of me, the shadows rising around

him made him look like the dark prince he truly was. "Make them release you, at the very least."

My jaw tensed and I let the frustration turn to anger. I needed this to work. I needed to have something that could make me stronger.

Focusing on the tendrils that were twisting around me, I urged them to ease their grip. I felt that little pull, that thread that seemed to connect me to his shadows. I held the sensation while I ordered the shadows to release me and I could feel them weakening. Before they could dissipate, I sent them to Ryvin.

They wound around his legs. His eyes widened in surprise a moment before the shadows pulled him to the floor.

I hurried to my fallen knife and grabbed it before moving to the fallen prince. He was propped up on his elbows, looking in surprise at his bound legs. I climbed onto his legs, straddling him before quickly moving my blade to his throat. "Got you."

He grinned, then gripped my arms, quickly turning us so I was on the ground and he was on top of me. The shadows faded like smoke being blown in a breeze and I was left breathless on the dusty floor, the prince pinning me in place.

I was still holding the knife this time, but he had my wrists in his hands, preventing me from using it. That didn't stop me from squirming under him, trying to break the grip and use my weapon.

He didn't have his full weight on my hips, despite the fact that he was straddling me and I was still struggling against him. Frustrated, I tried to get my arms free, but he held fast. He watched me with an amused expression.

Grunting, I tried again, annoyed by how easy this was for him. It reminded me of just how much stronger he was than me. Just how much stronger everyone was than me.

The little flair of darkness returned, and I latched onto it, letting a smirk form on my own lips as I called to his magic. The shadows built behind him, then wrapped around his waist, pulling him off me.

He landed on the ground with a gasp.

I rolled over, then scrambled over to him, again climbing on top of him to pin him down. This time, the shadows helped me and when he tried to reach for me, he was unable to lift his arms.

"Not so fun being immobile, is it?" I asked.

"That depends on what you're going to do with me while you've got me here," he teased.

I rolled my eyes, then climbed off him. Just as I was re-sheathing my knife, the shadows found me and tugged me down. I cried out as I hit the floor, more from my bruised pride than actual pain. At least he'd had his shadows put me down softly.

"You celebrated your victory too soon," he said as he knelt down next to me.

I sat up. "I thought we were finished."

He lifted a brow. "How did you do that?"

"Do what?"

"I was still holding you down. You broke out effortlessly." He looked impressed.

I looked down at my arms and legs, which had been wrapped in dark tendrils moments ago. "I'm not sure."

"Maybe we need to make sure you're not overthinking

when you use my magic. You've got to stop blocking out your intuition. Let your instincts guide you more," he advised.

"My instincts have a history of making bad choices." I swept my leg out behind him, sending him down. He tumbled forward, landing on top of me.

Laughter bubbled up as I lay sprawled out on the floor, Ryvin on my stomach. He laughed, the sound deep and rich. I wasn't sure I'd ever heard him laugh before.

As we caught our breath, he pushed himself up until his face was hovering above mine. My chest felt like it was expanding with pure joy just from seeing the light in his eyes and the smile on his lips. Suddenly, the smile melted away, his expression taking on a different look. One I knew intimately.

I sucked in a breath as my whole body heated, and I tilted my chin in anticipation. That was all the invitation he needed.

When our lips met, it was an explosion.

27

ARA

I NEEDED THIS. I needed him. It didn't matter if things were complicated. There was no way of knowing if I'd ever solve things between us. All I knew was that this felt right for now. The taste of him, the feel of his body against mine, the fire I felt rising inside me... It made me feel more alive than I had in a long time.

I pulled away, panting and flushed. "Not here."

He ran a hand through his hair, then nodded. I stood, then offered my hand. He accepted, following me wordlessly as we left. I was grateful for the minimal guards. We only passed two, and both of them averted their gazes the second they saw us.

I struggled to open my door when we arrived, I was so flustered and overwhelmed with desire. Ryvin opened it and as soon as it closed behind us, his mouth was on mine again.

Shadows billowed up around us and I broke from the

kiss, taking in the swirling tendrils. Ryvin turned my chin so I was facing him. "Someone's emotions are getting the better of her."

"That's me again?" I asked as my fingers toyed with the edge of his tunic.

He smiled. "That's all you." He lifted his hand and hundreds of floating gold sparks joined the shadows, swirling and floating with the darkness. It was like being surrounded by stars.

I swallowed hard. "That's beautiful."

His eyes locked on me, his stare hungry. "Yes, it is." He cupped my cheek with his large hand. "Ara, I…"

I pressed my index finger to his lips. "Don't say anything. This is just sex."

His brow furrowed for a heartbeat before he nodded.

"This doesn't change anything." I wasn't sure if I was saying it for him or if I was reminding myself.

"Whatever you need," he said.

"Right now, I need you." I rose to my toes and threw my arms over his shoulders before slamming my lips into his. His hands moved to my back and my head, tangling in my hair. He returned my kiss eagerly. We devoured each other, desperate and messy. Our tongues clashed and we nipped and licked as we continued the onslaught. It was angry and frantic. As if we knew this might be our last chance.

The sound of tearing fabric competed with the sounds of our gasping breaths. My nipples peaked at the sudden exposure as my clothes fell to the ground. I reached for his tunic, yanking it up while trying to keep my lips locked to his.

He pulled away and I stood there, naked and panting. With a smirk, he removed his tunic and trousers then scooped me up. He stepped over my torn clothing as he carried me over to my desk.

I sat with my legs hanging over the side, hungrily taking in the man in front of me. He moved between my thighs, his large hands running up and down my skin. A moan escaped my lips unbidden. Even this simple touch was enough to make me feel like I was on fire.

His hands grasped my ass, pulled me to the edge so I was positioned against him. The shadows wove around us, mingling with the dazzling lights sparkling and floating. I'd seen his magic cause so much harm, but this was soft, comforting, protective. The swirling tendrils moved on phantom breezes, twisting and churning around us; pulsing and flowing like breath.

"You are so fucking beautiful," Ryvin said, his words breathy. He caressed my cheek, then slid his hand behind my head, pulling my face closer to him. "I will do anything to deserve you again."

My stomach tightened. I wasn't ready to explore the future of our relationship right now. I just needed to feel something good. I needed him. Even if I couldn't explain what that meant. "Ryvin..."

He groaned. "My name on your lips is the sweetest sound."

"If you don't kiss me, so help me..." I set my hands on his shoulders, then slid my hands lower, digging my fingers into his muscular arms.

He leaned down, his lips brushing against mine in the ghost of a kiss. He lingered there, our lips barely touching while tension built and frustration coiled. I lifted my chin, but he moved just enough to keep me from pressing my lips to his.

Just when I thought I might scream, he resumed the kiss. Gentle, exploring, passionate. This kiss was the opposite of what we'd started with. It was promises and hope; tenderness and peace. It was all the things we could be if we lived in another time or another place. If we were just two people who weren't tied to destinies beyond our control.

A tear slipped down my cheek and I tasted the salt. He pulled away, then wiped the tear with his thumb. It was too much. Too intimate and too real. I breathed in staccato breaths, trying to reconcile the rising emotions. I should stop him before my body made promises my heart couldn't match.

His fingers lifted my chin and his thumb traced my lower lip. "I know."

My heart thundered as our eyes met. Those words meant more to me than anything anyone had ever said. They were loaded. So much had passed between us, and more was coming our way.

When he pressed his lips to mine, I didn't fight it. I leaned into him as the gentle kiss built into something more powerful. We were in a rhythm, releasing all the desire and frustration. His hands caressed my back, holding me close as he entered me slowly.

I held my breath as my body adjusted to him, gasping when he pushed completely inside. I tilted my head, breaking the kiss; my back arched, strong hands holding me upright. He thrust into me and I wrapped my legs around his hips, pulling him closer.

I kissed his chest and his collarbone before making my way back to his mouth. He lifted me from the desk, carrying me to the bed, where he lay me down gently. I pressed my palm to his chest, preventing him from lowering his face to mine. His brows furrowed.

"My turn," I said, pushing him away from me. With a smirk, I was on my knees in front of him. He lifted his eyebrows. I climbed onto his lap, straddling him, then leaned forward, making him lie flat on the bed.

His cock was against me, and I teased him, lifting and lowering my hips against him. He groaned, then gripped my hips, moving along with me. I leaned down, kissing him deeply. His hands slid along my ass, then moved up my back, and into my hair. Then he rolled so I was under him again.

"Not fair," I teased.

"You were taking too long," he said with a growl. He moved lower, so his knees were between my legs. Then his fingers brushed over the sensitive nub between my thighs and I gasped, my hips rising in surprise.

When his mouth replaced his fingers, I cried out. He moved his tongue in expert motions, sending tingles that made me moan. Fingers entered me and I gripped the sheets as my back arched. The dual sensation made pressure build low in my belly, tightening like a spring wound too tight. Gasping and moaning, my hips bucked as he continued to work his mouth and fingers. Wetness grew and I knew I was about to come undone. Breathless and hot, I closed my eyes, letting the pleasure rise until it reached a crescendo, sending me over the edge with a scream.

Panting and spent, I took a moment to catch my breath while Ryvin watched me with pure pride in his expression. He lowered his head, ready to please me again, but I pulled away. "Now, it really is my turn."

"I want to make you scream again," he said.

"You will," I promised as I sat. I called the shadows, and they wrapped around the prince.

He laughed.

I commanded them to push him to the bed and, to my surprise, they obliged. As the shadows dissipated, I climbed on top of him. This time, I didn't hesitate and as I lowered myself on him and I watched as his eyes rolled into the back of his head.

Ryvin groaned, his breathing coming out in gasps as I lifted and lowered myself onto him. He dug his fingers into my hips, moving with me as I rode him.

I leaned down, kissing him as I continued to move my body. He gripped my ass, squeezing and caressing, before his hands explored the rest of me. My breasts pressed against his chest and the feel of his skin against mine was everything I needed. Pleasure rose with each grind of my hips, escalating along with my breath. When his arms closed around me, embracing me against him, I fell, my body leaping from the edge, pure bliss exploding through me. I moaned and cried out just as he found his own release.

Panting and satisfied, I climbed off him, then lay on the bed beside him, staring up at the twinkling gold lights. The few remaining shadows dissipated, fading as I came down from the high of my climax. I looked over at Ryvin. He was staring at me. "I think I like teaching you to use my shadows."

I chuckled. "I think I like it, too."

"You know, I might be up for a little more training," he said, lifting a suggestive brow.

My insides tightened in anticipation and I turned onto my side so I could face him. "I probably should practice more."

"I think you—" Ryvin turned, facing the door before he finished his sentence. The knock sounded a heartbeat later.

"This better be good," Ryvin growled.

"The dragons are arriving," Vanth called through the closed door.

My shoulders slumped. "We'll be right there."

28

ARA

EVERY HAIR on my body was on edge as I stared at the sky. Even in the darkness, I could see the wings flapping above us.

Dozens of dragons circled Athos, their monstrous forms sending shivers down my spine. How had I ever thought I could fight these creatures?

"Makes you question everything, doesn't it?" Aunt Katerina asked.

I glanced over at her, noting that she still had her gaze skyward, watching as our new allies joined us.

She'd been away the last few days to meet the rest of our soldiers who were coming from the wall. Something about concern they'd see dragons flying along the route and attack if she wasn't there to assure them of our new alliance. Our soldiers from the wall were settling into their new barracks and recovering from their journey. Now, the dragons were here, searching for open spaces to land so they could join their king.

If Laera's estimate was correct, we'd see the red sails of Konos tomorrow. I glanced at the moon. Istvan had started tracking it as soon as the sky went dark and had explained it to me yesterday. I'd begrudgingly complimented him on his efforts and he'd invited me to come see the progress for Nyx's new temple. I wasn't sure how I felt about striking a tentative alliance with the priest.

The Dragon King stepped forward, Lagina by his side. I noted that both Cora and Sophia were not in attendance. Laera and Vanth had stayed behind as well, working with our soldiers to help them prepare for tomorrow's battle.

"You should go up there," Ryvin whispered.

Formal royal duties were the thing I tried to avoid more than anything, but Lagina could probably use the support.

I looped my arm through Ryvin's and dragged him along with me. It felt oddly familiar and comfortable to walk with him like this, but I meant what I said yesterday. Just because we gave into lust, didn't mean I was committing to anything. Despite the fact that we had dragons joining us, there was still a possibility I wouldn't live long enough for a decision about my relationship with Ryvin to matter, anyway.

The dragons were landing in the distance, then transforming back into men before walking toward us. From where I stood, I couldn't see the agonizing crunching of bones as their bodies shifted from one form to the other. It looked less painful, more organic. Perhaps it didn't hurt them the way it appeared to when I'd watched shifters change.

"Your men do know we are not enemies, correct?" Lagina

asked, her eyes following a massive brown dragon as it circled the sky above the landing area.

"They are honorable," he replied.

"Our men will follow our examples," Aunt Katerina said. "Friendship can be forged later. For now, I'm fine with us not killing each other."

The Dragon King chuckled. "If my bride's reluctance to our bond is any indication, it's going to take something very powerful to see friendship ever arise."

"She'll come around," Lagina said.

"How many dragons?" Ryvin asked, changing the subject.

"Five hundred arrive today," the king replied. "The rest of my forces are guarding Drakous."

"We'd have more soldiers, but we lost several hundred men during the Choosing." Aunt Katerina threw an annoyed look at Ryvin.

"I will not apologize for that," Ryvin said.

"Can we not right now?" I hissed.

A dozen men approached, ending our conversation. More dragons circled, and a steady stream of the Dragon King's men walked toward us as they continued to land and shift into their human form. Each of them stopped in front of their king, dropping to one knee in submission before continuing on toward the gathering area behind us.

One of the men lingered behind, staying on his knee after the others had left. "Your highness, I offer my life and my soul to your service."

"Get up, Kabir." The king shook his head. "So dramatic."

Kabir stood, a wide grin on his face, then he moved closer to the king. The two men embraced, the king slapping the other man on the back. "It's good to see you, brother."

Kabir was slightly shorter than his brother, but had the same dark red hair and wide, muscular form. Now that I was looking at him, I was surprised I hadn't put it together the moment I saw him.

When they separated, Lagina stepped forward. "Welcome, Prince Kabir."

"No need for a title, your highness," Kabir announced. "I'm never taking that throne. It could go right to Tatiana if anything ever happens."

"There's more of you?" I asked.

Kabir laughed. "Four of us. Something we have in common with the Athos royals, I think."

"Well, thank you for coming to our aid, Kabir," Lagina said. "You're welcome to call me Lagina."

"I'm on a first name basis with a queen, did you hear that, Bahar?" Kabir teased as he punched his brother in the arm.

"Bahar?" Lagina tested out the name and I stared at the king, as if seeing him for the first time. It was so strange realizing I'd never actually known his name. It seemed to familiarize him a bit, made him seem less of a threat.

The king, Bahar shrugged. "You never asked."

Lagina hummed. "You're right."

"Always so formal, this one," Kabir said, then turned his attention to me. "And you must be the lovely Ara I've heard so much about. The one who stole away the Fae Prince." He took my hand and kissed it before glancing at Ryvin, then returned his gaze to me. "Well done, darling."

"I'm not sure who stole who, if I'm being honest," I replied.

Ryvin lifted a brow.

"Well, your prince is a lucky man." Kabir released my hand, then inclined his head to Ryvin. "Your highness."

"Ryvin is fine."

"I think I might like it here. All this time, I heard about how formal and restrictive the Athos court was. But you've got a sister in love with the Fae Prince, another mated to a dragon, and one who just happens to be a vampire." Kabir smiled, as if fully amused by his own words. "I can't wait to see what secrets are revealed about you, my queen."

Lagina sighed. "I'm the boring one."

"Not at all. Ruler of the last human city? I'd say that counts for something," he said.

All this time, the king was half-focused on greeting the dragons who were continually trickling in, kneeling, then taking their leave. Behind us, a group of almost a hundred were gathered, awaiting orders.

"That's enough flattery and courtly manners for now, brother," Bahar said. "I need my general back."

"You're a general?" The words came out before I could stop myself.

"Don't let the playful attitude deceive you," Ryvin said. "He's got a reputation nearly as dark as my own."

"Thank you for that acknowledgement, kind sir," Kabir said with a flourish of his hand.

"I'll go with you," Aunt Katerina volunteered. "We can start getting your men settled."

Kabir and Aunt Katerina left us to take the dragons to their temporary housing. We'd gathered as many tents and supplies as we could, leaving them in the gardens for the dragons. Athos was not prepared to house so many warriors and there was no way we could send them into town. The people were likely terrified enough as it was. Istvan had sent envoys to each temple to help spread the news, but after everything we'd endured, it was going to be difficult to gain all their support.

Finally, the last of the dragons arrived and Lagina and Bahar were finished greeting the newcomers.

"I think you two should leave an offering for Nyx at the new temple site," Lagina announced as we walked toward the palace.

"The fae arrive tomorrow," I argued. "There has to be more important things for me to help with."

"You freed her from her prison, she might listen to you," Lagina said. Then she turned to Ryvin. "And you, well... there's a chance you could get through to her."

"The gods have never cared what their children thought of them," Ryvin replied.

"I know. But the two of you are our best chance at gaining any kind of sympathy," she said.

VATS OF OIL burned as the few workers dug and prepared the site for the temple to come. It was a beautiful location, a hill overlooking the palace. Certainly a place of honor.

"Will she even know if we leave offerings while she sleeps?" I asked Ryvin.

"I'm not sure," he admitted. "But she knew she was being ignored while trapped in that cave. Maybe they feel it somehow? I've never asked any of them about that."

"We should have asked Dion." I laughed. "Can you imagine his response?"

Ryvin smiled. "I'm pretty sure he considers every time someone has a glass of wine to be a tribute to him."

"It kind of is, I suppose," I said.

"Don't tell him that. He'd let that get to his head."

"I'm not sure that could make his ego any bigger than it already is," I replied with a smirk.

"You know, I would rather not see you with Dion, but if you wanted to be with him or someone else..." Ryvin started.

I set my hand on his arm. "Don't finish that sentence."

Istvan was walking toward us, the priest wearing a huge grin as he approached. "You came to see the progress."

"And to leave an offering for the goddess," Ryvin added, indicating the crate he held.

"Let me show you where the Naos will be," Istvan offered, leading us into the dirt.

Right now, it didn't look like much, but the fact that they were already toiling to make it into a temple in the darkness was impressive. That had to make an impact on Nyx. Hopefully, enough that she'd give us another chance.

We stopped in the center of a flattened dirt space. "This will be the heart of the temple. We already have interested acolytes who would like to pledge their lives to the goddess."

"That's...wonderful," I bit out. While I couldn't see myself locked away in a temple, I knew there were some who chose that path. If it was truly a choice, I applauded their passion.

Ryvin set down the crate and pulled out a bottle of wine, offering it to the priest. "Would you care to say some words to the goddess?"

Istvan smiled as he reached for the bottle and my insides twisted. It was such a slimy, disconcerting expression.

Ryvin handed me a pot of honey, then took the bottle of olive oil for himself. I waited as Istvan uncorked the bottle, then lifted it skyward. "Great goddess of night and sky, thank you for the gift of extended starlight and the chance to appreciate the beauty of darkness. We welcome your return and give homage to you. Please accept our offerings as our way of thanking you for all you give." He poured the wine into the soil.

Ryvin lifted his bottle. "To the honored goddess." He poured the oil onto the ground.

I hesitated for a moment, wondering if Nyx knew what was in our heads, or if she could only hear what we spoke. Realizing I wasn't even sure if she was going to hear anything while she slumbered, I lifted the honey. "To the goddess of night."

I tipped the jar and watched the honey slowly pour toward the ground. As I waited for the slow-moving substance to empty from the jar, I realized the surrounding area was silent.

The shovels had ceased. The chatter had stopped. I looked up and noted that we were alone. Only the occasional crackle of the flames punctuated the silent night.

"Where is everyone?" I asked.

Ryvin pulled his sword from its sheath just as we were surrounded.

29

ARA

I DROPPED the jar I was holding and reached for my knife, turning toward the approaching attackers. "What is this? Who are you people?"

They were dressed in black from head to toe, exactly like the group who'd shown up on our ship. Masks covered their faces, leaving only their eyes exposed. Lightning flashed and thunder rumbled. I risked a quick glance up and noticed that clouds had covered the stars.

These were definitely the same group we'd encountered before. Even down to the storms. What kind of magic were they summoning and how did they know we'd be here?

The group parted, allowing one of their own through with a struggling Istvan in their grip. I lifted a brow, wondering if they honestly thought I'd be willing to do anything in exchange for the priest. It made me a terrible person, but I was glad it was him this time and not me.

"Let me go," Istvan hissed through gritted teeth. He struggled against the grip of the man approaching us, but it just seemed to make the stranger annoyed. I swear I saw him roll his eyes.

"What do you want from us?" Ryvin asked as he moved closer to me.

"We're here for you, princeling. And we aren't going to stop hunting you until we have you," the man holding Istvan said with a growl.

The hair on my neck stood. I was certain it was the same voice I'd heard before. I'd watched them toss their bodies into the sea, but that didn't mean anything.

"You have no reason to be holding me," Istvan said. "I'm an old man, a priest. The gods will punish you if you harm me."

"The gods already have punished me," the man said. "And I wouldn't be here without your invitation."

I narrowed my eyes. "You told them we were here? You sold us out?"

"I will always do what is best for Athos. You have been a curse on this kingdom since the day you were dropped at the palace gates," Istvan sneered.

Shadows billowed around me, spreading from my feet. I knew I'd summoned them and when I glanced over at Ryvin, the pride in his expression was unmistakable.

Suddenly, the sky opened, and rain poured down, snuffing the torches and making the vats of oil flicker and sizzle. My clothes were soaked through in an instant. I felt the magic leave abruptly as my focus turned to the downpour.

"Last warning. You can come with us freely, or we kill the

priest, then we kill you and your girl," the man holding Istvan hollered.

"Go ahead and kill him. You can't have the prince." I took a step in front of Ryvin. There was no way I would let them near Ryvin. Last time we'd encountered this group, I'd almost lost him to a poison we didn't have another antidote for.

"How can you take the side of Konos over your home?" Istvan hissed.

"You are not my home," I snapped.

The assassin dragged his blade over Istvan's throat and the priest made a choking sound. I tensed, guilt rushing in. Not because I felt bad for Istvan, but because I felt like the world was a better place without him. I wasn't any better than the enemies I fought. The priest was right, I wasn't sure I could call Athos home with thoughts like mine.

Blood ran from the wound and bubbled from his mouth. He gagged and sputtered, sucking in desperate breaths before his body went limp.

The killer tossed the body aside as if he were nothing more than an annoyance. He wiped the blade on his tunic casually. Calmly, he looked up at us. "I will not miss out on this bounty again."

I held my knife in front of me, overly aware of the fact that we were surrounded. There were at least six men in a circle around us. I'd lived through worse odds and so had Ryvin. "This is your last chance to leave here unharmed."

The assassin laughed, then he lunged. I dodged, then swiped with my blade, missing my attacker. He charged for me again, moving with frightening speed. If I hadn't trained with Laera, I wouldn't have seen anything like this. I heard the grunting and clashing of bodies and blades as Ryvin fought enemies of his own, leaving me with the leader.

My assailant moved with ease, despite the wet ground. My feet slid in the mud, and my hair was falling in front of my face, but I couldn't risk pushing it away.

I managed to make contact, my blade catching fabric but not breaking skin. The assassin grinned. "You're feistier than I remember."

"You're struggling to kill a human," I shot back.

He shoved me and I stumbled back, my heels hitting something that knocked me to the ground. I landed on Istvan's body and panic flared. Before I could get to my feet, the assassin had his foot on my chest, pressing me down on top of the dead priest. "What was that you were saying, Princess?"

I rolled away, ending up face down, staring Istvan right in his lifeless eyes. The weight of the foot returned, this time on my back. I grunted and tried to roll away again, but this time I was pinned.

Cool steel pressed against my cheek. "I really should stop toying with you when we meet and just kill you. But where's the fun in that?"

"What did I ever do to you?" I asked.

"You were spared, while so many others weren't," he said. "You aren't even supposed to be alive, daughter of Ceto."

Ryvin slammed into the assassin and knocked him from me, sending him to the ground. I scrambled off of Istvan, my feet sliding in the mud as I did, making it take longer than it should for me to stand.

When I finally regained my footing, I spun to find Ryvin facing off with the only remaining fighter. It was too familiar.

Too much like last time. Fear and anger heated my insides, bringing something else along with them. That thread of magic, but this time, it was different. Tangled and messy. I didn't care. All I knew was that I had to do something.

I moved forward and my sandals stuck to the mud. Kicking them aside, I continued bare foot, making my way toward Ryvin and the last assassin.

I stopped close to them, tracking them, trying to isolate the attacker. They were so close, I was concerned I'd make a mistake and harm Ryvin. I took a deep breath, then I closed the distance and I shoved Ryvin to the ground before releasing everything I could.

The rain froze in the air, the droplets hovering like balls of glass. Then they collided, twisting and spinning in a cyclone laced with darkness. No, not darkness, shadows.

Water and shadows twisted around the assassin, tightening around him in sparkling dark ribbons. He cried out, struggling against the restraints. Jaw tense, I pushed the magic, commanding it to continue its onslaught. It formed a strange cocoon around our attacker until he was submerged in water and shadows. The magic twisted and churned, wrapping and spinning around him in a whirlwind.

"That's enough," Ryvin called.

It wasn't enough. I was convinced this was the same person who'd nearly killed him.

"I said, that's enough," Ryvin shouted.

I couldn't stop. I had to make sure the assassin couldn't harm us again.

Ryvin's hand touched my arm and I started, losing hold of the magic. Water rushed down, crashing like a waterfall as it hit the ground. The assassin was gone.

The rain stopped just as suddenly as it had arrived. My knees gave out and Ryvin caught me. He smoothed back my hair, then tilted my chin so I was looking up at him. "You are fucking amazing. Did you know that?"

I was too tired to respond, but I managed a chuckle.

"Let's get you back so you can rest. We're going to need those new skills against my father's army." He scooped me up, and I leaned against his warm chest.

He felt like home.

30

ARA

I WALKED into the palace on my own.

"I think you should rest," Ryvin suggested.

"Soon," I assured him. We'd been silent on our return, but I knew he had questions and was likely concerned about the amount of magic I'd used. I had questions of my own. The greatest one was if tapping back into my own magic through Ryvin put me back on the gods' radar. And not in a good way. Though, I was growing more certain by the day that things were never good if the gods noticed you at all. Even if my magic wasn't upsetting them, I felt like I was running on borrowed time.

A small figure appeared in the hallway, her ethereal form coming around the corner almost made it seem like she'd materialized from thin air. Maybe she had.

"Morta," Ryvin stopped next to me. "What are you doing here?"

"You thought you could get away with it?" she asked.

"I knew it," I murmured under my breath. I'd saved us and doomed us all at the same time.

"Not you, girl. Though, I'm sure they'll notice what you did soon enough. For now, they're distracted," Morta said.

"I thought the gods enjoyed when mortals fought," Ryvin said.

"The magic," she clarified. "That magic in the cave. You released it. It's going to have consequences beyond your imagination. Even I didn't see that coming."

"Take that up with my father. He's the one who trapped it there in the first place," I pointed out.

"Because someone asked him to," Morta said. "Keeping humans free of magic makes them vulnerable. Easier to manipulate. Weak."

"You're joking, right?" I asked.

"Now I understand why your path was so unclear," Morta said. "You are a catalyst."

My brow furrowed. "I don't understand."

"It isn't necessarily what you do, but it's the things you set in motion for those around you," she said. "You inspire people. Embolden them. You bring change. If I didn't know who your mother was, I'd wonder if you were born of the muses."

"Are you saying I make people do bad things that cause us trouble?" I asked.

"You weren't supposed to live," she said, her tone wispy and high-pitched. "And if your mother had sent you to the Underworld, as she did with her other children, you wouldn't have set these things in motion." She glanced at Ryvin. "You would have no mate and you'd still be your father's right hand."

Ryvin moved closer to me. "Why are you here, Morta?"

She smiled, the sight disturbing. "Because I want to watch as it all crumbles. I gambled when I let her live. And I want to see the payoff."

"We're going to lose," I said, the words tumbling out through numb lips.

"Probably," she agreed. "There are many possibilities. And most of them are not good for you. But there is a chance that what you do tonight will change the whole world."

"I know you better than that," Ryvin said. "What are you leaving out? It's not like you to give me such cryptic messages. That's better suited to your sisters."

She hesitated, then glided closer to us. The sheer gray fabric of her peplos floating around her made her look even more weightless.

I tensed as she stopped right in front of us. I'd never stood this close to her, and I could feel the magic radiating from her in waves. It made my stomach churn.

"My sisters are on their way." Morta turned her attention to me. "You know what that means, girl?"

I held my breath, then shook my head, not sure how to interpret what she'd just said. Was she threatening me or warning me?

"It means the gods are watching what happens in Athos," she said.

"I don't understand," I managed. None of what she was saying was helpful.

"It means your fates are all connected now. What happens here will impact all of us," she replied. "You have managed to disrupt the very stars, and I can't wait to see how this ends."

The fate spun, turning away from us. Then she glided down the hall, leaving us standing there.

"What just happened?" I asked.

"That was a warning," Ryvin said.

"She didn't explain anything," I countered. "What exactly was she warning about?"

"You can't fight tomorrow," he said after a long silence.

I shot a glare at him. "You think keeping me locked away in the palace is going to stop the gods from finding me?"

He sighed. "No."

"Then we do what we have planned. I will help you and Laera find your father. It's the only chance we have," I said.

"I can't lose you," he sounded pained.

"You aren't going to lose me. I can fight. Hiding me away to wait for them to find me is only going to prolong the inevitable if it's my time," I said.

He closed the distance between us. "This is killing me, Ara. I feel like I already lost you. You and me, with this distance between us. I know I deserve it. I know it's my fault. I need more time. I can't lose you before I prove that I deserve you."

I reached for him, sliding my hand behind his head, my fingers weaving into his dark hair. "You never really lost me. I don't know what the future holds, or if the fates would ever allow us to be happy, but I do know I can't imagine any future where you're not by my side."

He leaned down and kissed me hard. His body pressed against me and I stumbled backward until I hit the wall.

Somehow, we managed to make it to a door, practically

falling into the first room we found. I closed the door behind us and scanned the darkened space. Ryvin sent an orb of light into the air, and I realized we were in the seamstress' room. Colorful fabrics were piled on tables. Baskets were scattered around, full of supplies. In the corner was the screen we used to change behind and in the center of the room was a pedestal we'd stand on for measuring.

The only thing I cared about was the fact that we were alone. And there was no way anyone was going to be working on any dresses tonight. I tugged on Ryvin's tunic, dragging him toward the long table. He was already unpinning the fibulae that held my peplos together at my shoulder. The fabric fell into a puddle around my feet and I stepped out of it. He lifted me so I was on the table, laying me down on the piles of silk and linen.

He'd removed his clothes and, with a mischievous smirk, climbed on top of the table, settling between my thighs. I lifted myself on my elbows so I could kiss him again and his arms wrapped around my back, holding me in an embrace as he entered me.

Our moments were frantic, as if we would be discovered at any moment. My back slid over the smooth silk with each thrust, and I moaned as he continued to move inside me.

Suddenly, the table shuddered, then collapsed, and I screamed, but I didn't hit the ground. Instead, I was in a hammock of shadows, hovering above the floor.

"How did you do that?" I asked, breathless.

The shadows lowered us gently until we were safely on the ground. "I told you, I'll always protect you."

I kissed him fiercely, giving in to all the complicated feelings. There was no way I would ever be able to stay away from him. And I realized I didn't want to.

Without breaking our kiss, he pulled me onto his lap. Our bodies fit together like a puzzle. He filled me so perfectly. I moved on top of him, undulating my hips, using my knees to lift and lower, driving myself closer and closer to the edge.

Our hands and mouths were a frenzy of touch and taste, the sensations driving me insane. I could feel him on every inch of me until I wasn't sure where I began and he ended.

My pace quickened along with my breathing. Ryvin's breath was hot on my neck. He groaned and I knew he was close. With a gasp, I let myself fall, let myself give in.

Pleasure erupted through me, sending shockwaves down my spine. My back arched and I cried out just as Ryvin found his own release.

When I caught my breath, I stared at him. My enemy; my dark prince; my lover; my mate. My whole world. "I love you." The words came out on their own, but I meant it, and I knew there was nobody else for me but him.

He pulled me close, wrapping his strong arms around me. He nuzzled into my neck and whispered, "I love you."

Somehow, we made it to my room and into my bed. If we were about to face death, I was going to spend every last moment feeling alive.

31

ARA

HORNS SOUNDED and I sat up, instantly feeling cold in all the places where Ryvin's arms had been. Lights hummed to life around my room, the floating orbs taunting me in the darkness.

The horn blared again, and I swung my legs off the bed only to be pulled back. Ryvin pressed his lips to mine in a hungry, almost painful kiss. Stubble scratched against my cheeks and I kissed him back, memorizing the movements for a moment before breaking free.

By the third horn blare, we were both up, pulling on our leathers. It didn't take long for us to join the others at the overlook on the top of the palace. People were streaming in through the gates, seeking sanctuary behind the palace walls. It was false comfort, but we weren't going to turn our people away. If there was any chance of surviving this, it was better not to be in the city.

The sea stretched into eternity, the ships sailing toward us barely visible in the darkness.

"He didn't bring his whole fleet," Laera said.

"Where did the rest of them go?" Ryvin asked. "You said he was bringing everyone here."

Laera looked over at her brother and I saw fear in her eyes. I didn't even know she could be afraid of anything. "He must know more about my power than we realized."

"He manipulated you?" I asked.

"What are you talking about?" Lagina asked.

"This isn't right. Something isn't right," Laera said.

"The dragons are going to be able to take these ships," Vanth said. "He knew, didn't he? He knew that Athos had dragons on their side."

"But he didn't know we'd free the magic," Laera said.

"Where are the rest of the ships? Are they coming later? Waiting for the first wave to distract us?" I asked.

Laera's eyes were closed and Ryvin lifted a finger, indicating that we should wait.

I looked toward the shore, barely visible in the dark. Vanth was down there with the rest of the ground forces, waiting for the few ships who made it past the dragon attack.

The bells tolled. It was time.

Dragons took to the sky, flapping their large wings as they raced toward the ships.

"We have to go," Ryvin said.

"Be careful, Ara," Lagina said.

I nodded, then looked to where Laera was still standing with her eyes closed. She was supposed to join us. The three of us would fight with our soldiers on land, doing whatever we could to protect them and take down any fae who made it here.

She opened her eyes, then sucked in a deep breath. "He used my magic against me."

"What do you mean?" Lagina asked. "What does this mean for Athos?"

She looked at my sister. "He's going after Drakous. This fleet is all a decoy."

Laera grabbed Ryvin's arm. "How did he fool me? Did you tell him? How does he know? I haven't even told my mother what I can do."

"I don't know," Ryvin said, then he glanced skyward. "But we have bigger problems right now."

A huge, winged beast flew above the Konos ships, the creature only visible from the silhouette it created as it blotted out the stars.

"That's one of ours, right?" Cora asked nervously.

Fire exploded from the beast's mouth, a warning blast aimed at the oncoming dragons.

"How the fuck did he get a dragon on his side?" Laera asked.

Another burst of flame shot across the sky, illuminating dozens of dragons flying toward Athos. Would the dragons on our side be able to take them down, or would they reach the city before they could stop them?

"Get inside!" I screamed. "Get everyone under cover." I pushed Cora forward and grabbed Lagina's arm. "Get out of here."

"Where did they come from?" Laera demanded.

"I don't know, but we have to get down there," I said.

Ryvin, Laera, and I made our way to where the soldiers

were waiting. Vanth was shouting orders, but I wasn't sure if anyone was listening. The rows of men in the blue tunics of Athos were staring skyward and some of them had broken ranks to move for a better view.

"Where do you want us, general?" Ryvin called to Vanth.

The shifter turned to us. "Where did those fucking dragons come from?"

"No idea. But I think we're going to see more fighters reaching shore than we anticipated," Ryvin said.

"This changes nothing," Vanth ordered, turning to address the men. "We fight for your city. Don't think about the dragons. Focus on making sure anyone who leaves one of those boats doesn't make it past the shore."

I clenched my hands into fists, working to contain the nervous energy that was making my insides twist and churn.

"This isn't just for our city," Nico, an older general who had served under my father, called. "This is for all humans. We will not allow the fae to have any say in our affairs. That ends now. Tonight."

He lifted his fist in the air and yelled. The men joined, crying out in unison. Cheers and screams echoed around us, their excitement sending away most of my nerves. They were right, this was for Athos. For all humans. We were going to save our city.

"For Athos!" Nico called, then he ran. The soldiers followed him, charging toward the shore where the boats had just made landfall.

I pulled my daggers from their sheaths, then nodded at Ryvin and Laera.

The prince gripped his sword. Shadows swirled around him, twisting around his wrists and ankles. "Let's find out if my father is brave enough to fight his own battles or if he went with the other ships to Drakous."

With causal steps, he walked forward, lifting his hand, he sent shadows slithering down the sand. Laera followed in his wake and I stayed a few steps behind them.

Bodies fell as we cut through the battle, shadows taking them out one by one as we passed. Fae in red tunics fell without effort. After our encounter with the assassins who withstood his powers, I'd forgotten just how dangerous he was. These weren't humans. These were fae. And Ryvin's shadows were calming them one by one, without concern.

I should have been afraid, but all I could do was think about how grateful I was that he was on our side.

As we neared the shore, I couldn't help but steal glances at the people fighting all around us. Sand flew, steel clashed, men cried out in agony as they were struck down.

I gasped, jumping back as a man in a blue tunic fell at my feet. Blood poured from a wound in his side. His eyes were open, staring blankly at the sky.

His killer stood over him, breathing heavily, gripping a blood-soaked sword. The red-clad Konos fighter smiled at me, revealing fangs. I lifted my knife and bared my teeth at him. I was really starting to hate vampires.

With a yell, the man charged me, his sword above his head. I dodged, then swept my foot under him, sending him to the ground. His sword fell from his grip and while he reached for it, I shoved my knife into his thigh, then removed it quickly. He screamed, his hands going to the injury automatically.

With a snarl, he pushed himself to standing, then landed a punch to my jaw. Pain shot through my face and my eyes watered. He lunged, throwing his arms around me, then knocked both of us to the ground.

Someone kicked him in the side, knocking him from me and I quickly moved away and got to my feet. Laera's foot was on the man's chest. "You were never the best fighter, Pete."

He grunted, then grabbed her leg, tugging so she lost her balance and was pulled to the side.

Rage made me feel too hot. Nobody treated my friends like this. Shadows billowed up around me, reaching for the soldier. They wrapped around his arms and legs, pulling him to the ground. His eyes widened. He cursed, then said something in a language I didn't recognize.

I closed my hand into a fist, ordering the shadows to smother the man. They obliged, surrounding him before squeezing in around him until there was nothing left but wisps of darkness where his body had been.

Laera spit on the place he'd been, then looked around. I did the same, gripping my knife again in case we had another attacker. The battle had shifted and we were on the edge, mostly ignored.

Laera grabbed my arm and pulled me farther from the fighting. "Ryvin isn't here."

I scanned the battlefield, struggling to make out individuals in the darkness. Only a few fae lights floated in the sky, keeping the fight in shadows.

"Where did the shadows come from, Ara?" she asked. "Was that you?"

"You already know the answer to that," I said, still scanning the fight for the prince.

Dragon fire shot across the sky, returned by an answering

stream of fire from one of the opposing dragons. The winged creatures were having a battle of their own in the air.

"Well, let's hope the gods don't see it as a threat," she said.

"The gods aren't exactly my concern right now." I was still trying to find Ryvin. "Where is your brother?"

She was scanning the fight now as well, both of us trying to find the prince. "There!"

I saw him just as she pointed him out and my heart dropped into my stomach. Ryvin was surrounded by a circle of fallen men and more were charging toward him. But that wasn't the reason I sprinted toward him. "Run, Ryvin!"

A massive dragon was unleashing fire on the soldiers fighting, and it was heading right for my prince.

32

BAHAR

THESE WEREN'T DRAGONS. I didn't know what they were, but it had to be sorcery. Something dark and dangerous. Something that shouldn't exist.

I led my dragons forward, our wings beating in the darkness, moving with practiced precision. We'd fought so many battles together over the years, but we'd never fought against this.

I unleashed fire, aiming at the creature coming our way. The beast screeched, a high pitched, bird-like sound. Kabir came beside me, launching a blast of his own flames at our opponent.

The creature flickered and shimmered, then burst into dust that scattered toward the earth. I glanced at my brother, his gold scales glinting in the moonlight. He gave me a look before turning his attention to the next creature.

I continued my path, diving lower to ignite one of the

ships waiting near the harbor. Arrows flew through the air and I turned, avoiding them with ease. Then another round of arrows came from the ship alongside the one I was charging. I beat my wings, rising above them, but one caught my wing, piercing the delicate membrane. I roared, then dove, aiming for the men who'd dared to shoot at a dragon.

With a burst of flame, the vessel caught fire. Men screamed and leaped over the edge and I knew the beasts of the sea would finish them for me. More arrows flew past and I turned, unleashing more fire on the second ship.

The rest of my dragons flew nearby, attacking the enemy dragons and ships. It was too easy, though, and there were too few ships. We'd expected all of Konos and all of the courts of Telos. This wasn't all of the Fae King's fleet.

I flew beyond the waiting ships, knowing there were more than enough from Drakous to take care of the enemies below. Scanning the dark water, I searched for hidden ships. They had to be out here, waiting for a signal. There had to be more.

My eyesight as a dragon made easy work in the dark. I could see everything. The occasional creature cut through the lapping waves, the island of Konos far in the distance, shrouded in eternal clouds.

What I didn't see were more ships.

I turned back toward Athos, anger simmering. We'd been betrayed. The Princess of Konos was well known for her network of spies. I'd trusted what she'd said, but she'd made fools out of all of us.

Taking out any ship I crossed, I headed to shore, knowing the others were getting easy target practice with the false dragons and practically empty ships.

Ahead, the battle raged on the shore, but even I could tell

it wasn't nearly as many soldiers as we expected. None of this was right.

I landed nearby just as one of the enemy dragons cut past one of my own. The creature opened its mouth and rained fire down on the battlefield.

33

ARA

RYVIN LOOKED over and our eyes met. I screamed, the sound swallowed by the din of the battle.

It was as if everything was moving in slow motion. I dodged sword strikes and weaved around fighters. Screams followed in the dragon's wake. The scent of charred flesh and brimstone filled my nostrils. I wasn't going to make it in time.

Something tore inside me. That dark thing I'd been fighting exploded, releasing every drop of fear; every feeling of rejection; all the times I'd felt weak or powerless. It burst free like lightning tearing through the clouds. Water rushed past me, a tidal wave roaring up from the nearby sea. It washed over the battlefield and crashed down on top of Ryvin just as the dragon passed by. The fire sizzled and steamed, protesting against the water.

The beast roared, but continued its path, flying toward Athos. The wave tugged me under as it receded, pulling me toward the sea. I swallowed great gulps of the salty water before I was able to right myself. Where the battlefield had been stood hundreds of confused and sopping wet soldiers. Bodies rushed past me, pulled out to the ocean with the wave.

I shivered against the cold of the icy water. Wading back toward shore, I fought against the push and pull of the tide, the waves splashing against my chest when they rolled back toward the sea.

Frantically, I searched for my friends. Where were they? The fighting had paused and there were a lot less soldiers on the shore.

"Ara!" Ryvin shouted.

"Ryvin?" I narrowed my eyes and found the waving figure in the darkness. I waved back. My shoulders sagged in relief. He was alright. As soon as I got to shore, I had to find Laera and Vanth. I needed to see them all, know they were safe.

Something slithered past my leg. I tensed, pausing my progress. I couldn't see the details in the black water, but I knew something large had joined me. I reached for the charm at my throat, my fingers brushing against the metal. I knew it would help me find Ceto's island and it was supposed to keep me safe, but did it work here?

The creature slithered past me again, and I moved to the side, bumping into more slick scales.

It was wrapped around me, holding me in place. My pulse raced. "I'm not going to harm you." Could the creature understand me?

I felt it move again, then I was lifted from the water, the creature under me. With a yelp, I wrapped my arms around its neck to keep from falling. As soon as I was holding onto it,

I felt more at ease. Suddenly, I knew the monster wasn't going to harm me.

It swam forward, toward shore, stopping when the water got shallower. It lowered its head, and I climbed off. In the few remaining lights, I could see the creature's face and its huge glowing gold eyes.

"Thank you," I said.

It whipped its head away from me and snapped its jaws. When I looked over, I saw feet dangling from the monster's upturned head and a pair of Konos soldiers were running.

The serpent crunched on its prey. The bones snapping before it tipped its head back and swallowed the man whole. My hands were shaking. This creature might have helped me, but it was dangerous.

Out of the corner of my eye, I noticed that one of the Konos boats was leaving. They were fleeing.

The serpent ducked back into the water, and I knew it was chasing the boat.

Above, dragon fire shot from the sky, engulfing another Konos ship that was making its way from Athos.

Cheers erupted from behind me, and I turned to see Ryvin watching me. Laera and Vanth were standing next to him. All of them were holding their weapons at their sides, their gazes fixed on the ships leaving Athos.

I walked toward them, shivering and soaking wet, but alive. "They're leaving."

"My father wasn't with them," Laera said. "This wasn't the real battle."

"Where did those dragons come from?" I asked.

"They weren't real dragons," she said. "It was magic. As soon as they faded, they started to retreat."

"They were testing it out on us," I said.

"Athos is an easier target than Drakous. This was a training run," Vanth said.

I looked to the sky where the dragons were still circling our shore. What were they going to say when they landed and realized what was happening?

"We have to help them," I said. "We can't let them take Drakous."

I noticed a group walking toward us and narrowed my eyes, trying to make them out. "It's the dragons."

We turned, watching as the king and many of his men walked toward us. Their bodies were tense, and I could almost feel their anger from here.

"You all have a lot of explaining to do before I light this entire city on fire," Bahar said with a growl. A trail of blood seeped down his bare arm. Several other shifters followed behind him, all of them back in their human form. Some were injured, like their king, others were simply windblown. They all wore cloth wrapped around their waists and matching angry expressions.

"They used my power against me," Laera said. "I don't know how, but he knew."

"This was a decoy, wasn't it?" Bahar asked.

"I think so," Laera confirmed.

"He's always wanted Drakous," Ryvin said.

"And his children used me to ensure he could attack my home while I was away with my best men, protecting a useless human city," Bahar snapped.

"That's not what happened," Ryvin said.

"Where is he now, Princess?" Bahar turned his attention to Laera. "Or have you conveniently lost your abilities?"

Laera shook her head. "I don't know. I don't know how he shut me out."

"Because you were in on it." Bahar moved with speed I didn't expect and grabbed me, pulling me away from my friends.

Stunned, I stumbled forward, then had to regain my balance. "What are you doing?" I yanked my arm, trying to free myself from his grip.

Ryvin pulled out his sword and took a step closer. "Release her now, shifter."

"Swear on her life that you didn't betray me," Bahar said.

Everyone was silent. All the Athos soldiers who'd formed a circle around us, all of Bahar's men, stared at us, waiting.

"I swear on her life," Ryvin said. "I'm telling you, we thought this was it. We thought we'd finally be free of him."

The Dragon King released me and I rushed to my friends, making sure I was out of his reach.

"Is he already in Drakous?" Bahar asked.

"I'm not sure," Laera said.

"We have to get home," Kabir said.

More dragons had arrived, falling into line behind their king. They whispered amongst each other, likely passing along the information to the newcomers.

"We'll go to Drakous," I said. "We'll help."

The king looked surprised, but before he could say anything, Vanth walked in front of him, staring at something behind us. "What is that?"

Confused, I turned, scanning the shore. "What are you talking about?"

He pointed skyward and I gasped. Murmurs and

surprised whispers rose up from everyone on the beach. The horizon was pink. The sun was rising.

"It looks like Nyx is awake," Ryvin said.

"We might have a bigger problem than my father," Laera said.

Nyx would be coming for Athos, but the Fae King was heading to Drakous. Morta had been right, the whole world was about to change. And there was very little chance we'd get out of this alive.

THANK YOU FOR READING! I can't wait to share what happens next with you in the final installment, *Queen of Serpents and Shadows.*

WANT MORE WHILE YOU WAIT? Get a bonus scene & updates from me by joining my newsletter! https://tinyurl.com/starsandfate

Go to my newsletter sign up

WHAT'S NEXT?

Find Book 4, Queen of Serpents and Shadows on Amazon

Also By Alexis Calder

Rejected Fate Series

Darkest Mate

Forbidden Sin

Feral Queen

Royal Mates Series

Shifter Claimed

Shifter Fated

Shifter Rising

Academy of Elites Series

Academy of Elites: Untamed Magic

Academy of Elites: Broken Magic

Academy of Elites: Fated Magic

Academy of Elites: Unbound Magic

Brimstone Academy Series

Brimstone Academy: Semester One

Brimstone Academy: Semester Two

Romcom books published under Lexi Calder:

In Hate With My Boss

Love to Hate You

ABOUT THE AUTHOR

Alexis Calder writes sassy heroines and sexy heroes with a sprinkle of sarcasm. She lives in the Rockies and drinks far too much coffee and just the right amount of wine.

Printed in Great Britain
by Amazon

59139960R00152